Henry Playford

Wit and Mirth or Pills to Purge Melancholy - Being a Collection of the Best Merry Ballads and Songs, Old and New...

Vol. II

Henry Playford

Wit and Mirth or Pills to Purge Melancholy - Being a Collection of the Best Merry Ballads and Songs, Old and New...
Vol. II

ISBN/EAN: 9783744762526

Printed in Europe, USA, Canada, Australia, Japan

Cover: Foto ©Andreas Hilbeck / pixelio.de

More available books at **www.hansebooks.com**

WIT and MIRTH:

OR

PILLS

TO PURGE

Melancholy ;

BEING

A Collection of the best Merry BALLADS
and S O N G S, Old and New.

Fitted to all Humours, having each their proper
T U N E for either Voice, or Instrument :
Most of the S O N G S being new Set.

VOL. II.

LONDON :

Printed by *W. Pearson*, for *J. Tonson*, at
SHAKESPEAR'S Head, over - against
Catherine Street, in the *Strand*, 1719.

DEDICATION.

TO the Right Honour-able the *Lords* and *Ladies;* and also to the Honoured *Gentry* of both kinds that have been so Generous to be *Subscribers* to this *Second* Volume of SONGS; which end with some *Orations* spoken by me in the *Theatre:* Which are

With

with the Copys of Verses, *Prologues* and *Epilogues*, most humbly Dedicated by

Your most Oblig'd,

And

Devoted Servant,

T. D'Urfey.

AN
Alphabetical TABLE
OF THE
SONGS and POEMS
Contain'd in this
BOOK.

An Alphabetical TABLE.

Forc'd

An Alphabetical TABLE.

Leave

An Alphabetical TABLE.

'Tis

An Alphabetical TABLE.

Ye

POEMS.

Pills to Purge Melancholy.

VOL. II.

CAPONIDES;

Or Lyrical remarks Made on the famous Signior Cavaliero Nico — Grimaldi, *Knighted by the Doge of* VENICE, *and Signior* Gallapo Frisco, Caprioli Frontini *the Horse: Made a Consul by the* Roman *Emperor* CALLIGULA. *Set to a Tune in the* OPERA *of* ANTIOCHUS.

OME blooming Honour get
By Valour, some by Wit,
And some have Titles met
   By the way of *Guinny;*
But two, most fam'd I shew,
  One long since, and one now,
Who if you don't allow,
   The Devil's in ye:
Of Creatures I discourse,
Who must your liking force:
They must your liking force,
As well as my discourse,
Calligula's fine Horse,
   And *Nicol*——
Ni, *hi, hi, hi, hi, hi, hi* —colini.

A Senator some say,
He made his Dapple grey,
For his *Italian* Neigh,
          A Crack-brain'd Ninny;
A *Doge* too, as appears
With Squeaking, caught by th' Ears,
Amongst the *Chevaliers*,
          Plac'd *Nico*——:
And as the Horse did bear,
That Honour many a Year,
For squaling Notes so Cleer,
As you shall seldom hear,
So does our Capon dear,
          Dear *Nicol*——,
De, *he, he, he, he, he, he* —*ear* Nicol——.

Yet Criticks bold and plain,
As Envy still will reign,
For Head and comely Main,
          Cry up *Frontini;*
They say for Shapes before,
Good qualitys some score,
He merits Honour more,
          Then *Nicol*——:
Besides *un autre* chose,
More blest they him suppose,
More blest they him suppose,
For tho' the Grooms give blows,
They have not cut out those,
          Like *Nicol*——,
Ni, *hi, hi, hi, hi, hi, hi* —colini.

But yet by Vocal strain,
And subtle dint of Brain,
'Mongst *English* Gentry vain,
          He gets the Penny,
He Trills, and Gapes, and Struts,
And Fricassee's the Notes,
Our Crew may crack their Gutts,
          They ne'er will win ye :

For

For Quavering like a Lark,
This rare disabled Spark,
Gets Ladies too i'th dark,
Who tho' 'tis bungling work,
Will hug this Knight of Mark,
　　Smooth *Nicol*——,
Ni, *hi, hi, hi, hi, hi,* —colini.

But now to cause our Woe,
Why Chanter will you go,
Fop Bounty still may flow,
　　And many a Guinny ;
You leave us, some do guess,
To Build a sumptuous place,
To Seat your Noble Race,
　　Like *Valentini :*
But tho' we to our shames
Have Paid ye in Extreams,
When e'er you leave the *Thames,*
To rowl on Ocean streams,
Pray don't you call us Names,
　　Sweet *Nicol*——,
Swee, he, he, he, he, he, heet Nicol.

A New SONG, *Inscrib'd to the brave Men of*
Kent, *made in Honour of the Nobility and
Gentry of that Renown'd and Ancient
County.*

WHEN *Harrold* was Invaded,
     And falling lost his Crown ;
And *Norman William* waded
     Through Gore to pull him down :
When Countys round with fear profound,
     To mend their sad Condition ;
And Lands to save, base Homage gave,
     Bold *Kent* made no Submission.

CHORUS.

Sing, sing in Praise of Men of Kent,
     So Loyal brave and free ;
'Mongst Britain's *Race, if one surpass,*
     A Man of Kent *is he.*

The hardy stout Free-holders,
     That knew the Tyrant near ;
In Girdles, and on Shoulders,
     A Grove of *Oaks* did bear :
Whom when he saw in Battle draw,
     And thought how he might need 'em ;
He turn'd his Arms, allow'd their Terms,
     Compleat with noble Freedom :
Then sing in Praise, &c.

And when by Barons wrangling,
     Hot Faction did Increase,
And vile Intestine Jangling,
     Had banish'd *England's* Peace,
The Men of *Kent* to Battle went,
     They fear'd no Wild confusion ;
But joyn'd with *York,* soon did the work,
     And made a blest conclusion :
Then sing in Praise, &c.

At Hunting, or the Race too,
    They sprightly Vigour shew ;
And at a Female Chase too,
    None like a *Kentish* Beau :
All blest with Health, and as for Wealth,
    By Fortunes kind embraces ;
A Yeoman grey shall o,t out-weigh,
    A Knight in other places :
Then sing in Praise, &c.

The Generous, Brave and Hearty,
    All o'er the *Shire* we find ;
And for the *Low-Church* Party,
    They're of the Brightest kind :
For King and Laws, they prop the Cause,
    Which *High-Church* has confounded ;
They love with height the Moderate right,
    But hate the Crop-Ear'd *Round-head :*
Then sing in Praise, &c.

The promis'd Land of Blessing,
    For our Forefathers meant ;
Is now, in right Possessing,
    For *Canaan* sure was *Kent :*
The Dome at *Knoll,* by Fame enroll'd
    The Church at *Canterbury ;*
The Hops, the Beer, the Cherrys here,
    May fill a famous Story.
Then sing in Praise of Kentish *Men,*
    So Loyal, Brave and Free ;
'Mongst Britain's *Race, if one surpass,*
    A Man of Kent *is He.*

An ODE *on Queen* MARY: *Set by Mr.* Henry
Purcell, *and the Notes to be found in his*
Orpheus Brittanicus.

HIGH on a Throne of glittering Ore,
   Exalted by Almighty fate ;
Out-shining the bright Jem she wore,
  The Gracious *Gloriana* sate.

The dazling Beams of Majesty,
'Too fierce for mortal Eyes to see ;
She veil'd, and with a smiling Brow
She taught th' admiring World below.

Since Vertue is the chiefest good,
  Gay Power should only be her Dress ;
Which often taints the purest blood,
  Free Conscience is the solid Peace.

Glory is but a Flattering dream
Of wealth, that is not, tho' it seem ;
False Vision whose vain Joys do make
Poor Mortals poorer, when they wake.

The fawning croud of Slaves that Bow,
  With praise could ne'er my Sence controul ;
Vast Pyramids of State seem low,
  So much above it sits my Soul.

She spoke, whilst Gods unseen, that stood
Admiring one so Great, so Good ;
Flew straight to Heaven, and all along,
Bright *Gloriana* was their Song.

Advice to the Ladies.

Ladies

Adies of *London*, both Wealthy and Fair,
  Whom every Town Fop is pursuing ;
Still of your Purses and Persons take care,
  The greatest Deceit lies in Wooing :
From the first Rank of *Beaux Esprits,*
  Their Vices therefore I discover,
Down to the basest Mechanick degree,
  That so you may chuse out a lover.

First for the Courtier, look to his Estate,
  Before he too far be proceeding ;
He of Court Favours and Places will prate,
  And settlements make of his Breeding :
Nor wear the Yoak with dull Country Souls,
  Who though they are fat in their Purses ;
Brush with Bristles and Toping full Bowls,
  Make Love to their Dogs and their Horses.

But above all, the rank Citizens hate,
  The Court, or the Country choose rather ;
Who'd have a Block-head that gets an Estate,
  By Sins of the Cuckold his Father :
The sneaking Clown all Intriguing does Marr,
  Like Apprentices Huffing and Ranting ;
Cit puts his Sword on without *Temple-Bar,*
  To go to *White-Hall* a Gallanting.

Let no spruce Officer keep you in awe,
  The Sword is a thing Transitory ;
Nor be blown up by the Lungs of the Law,
  A World have been cheated before you :
Soon you will find your Captain grown bold,
  And then 'twill be hard to o'ercome him ;
And if the Lawyer touch your Copy-hold,
  The Devil will ne'er get it from him.

Fly, like the Plague, the rough Tarpawling Boys,
  That Court you with lying Bravadoes ;
Tiring your Senses with Bombast and Noise,
  And Stories brought from the *Barbadoes ;*

                                        And

And ever shun the Doctor, that Fool,
  Who seeking to mend your condition ;
Tickles your Pulse, and peeps in you Close-stool,
  Then sets up a famous Physician.

But if your Humour have such roving fits,
  As must upon Wedlock be treating ;
Step to *Will's Coffee House* you'll find some Wits,
  Who live upon Sharping and Cheating :
They wear good Cloaths, and Powder their Whiggs,
  And Swear y'are a Dear and a Honey ;
And their whole Lives spend in rampant Intrigues,
  Oh, they are the Men for my Money.

Advice to the Beaus ; *To the foregoing Tune.*

ALL Jolly Rake-hells that Sup at the *Rose*,
    And Midnight Intrigues are contriving ;
Courtiers, and all you that set up for *Beaus*,
  I'll give ye good Councel in Wiving ;
Now the fair Sex, must pardon my Verse,
  If once I dare swerve from my Duty ;
Old *Rosa crucians*, found spots in the Stars,
  Then why not I Errors in Beauty.

Shun the Cits Daughter whom a Gentleman got,
  Whilst he the Old Cause was revenging ;
Bred up at School to Sing, Dance, and wot not,
  Yet walks as she mov'd with an Engine :
Nor be by the *Orphans* Treasure provok'd,
  The Chamber is empty you see, Sir ;
Ne'er hope to keep a fine Cabinet lock'd,
  When every Furr'd Gown has a Key, Sir.

The

The Country Nymph that looks fresh as a Rose,
  Whose Innocent Grace does o'er rule ye;
Hobbles in Gate, and treads in with her Toes,
  Ah, take a great care least she fool ye:
She looks as if she knew not what's what,
  Yet bring her to Town to a Play, Sir;
Soon you'll perceive, that she'll fall from her Trott,
  And Modishly come to her Pace Sir.

The Buxom Widdow with Bandore and Peak,
  Her Conscience as black as her Cloathing;
If in a Corner you ever make Squeak,
  I'll give you her Joynture for nothing:
She still will plague ye with her Law smiles,
  She'll answer your Court by Attorney;
If you love riding in others old Boots,
  For God's sake make hast with your Journey.

But above all Sirs, despise the *Coquett,*
  She'll Sacrifice Love to Ambition;
Who takes a Wife that but thinks she's a Wit,
  Is in a most woful condition:
She'll make her Conscience stretch like her Glove,
  And now, tho' she vows equal Passion;
Perjur'd next moment, forswear all her Love,
  And make a meer Jest of Damnation.

The Maids of Honour, like fortifi'd Towns,
  Will give you Repulse if you venture;
Bulwark'd by Vertue and stiff bodied Gowns,
  The Devil himself cannot enter:
But if by Love's dear Bribe you get in,
  And for fatal Wedlock importune;
If you don't straight go to Law with the *Queen,*
  You'll ne'er get one Groat of their Fortune.

But if your Zeal for a Wife be so strong,
  That nothing can cool the fierce Passion,
Step to the *Rose,* and steal out Mrs. *Long,*
  She'll make the best Spouse in the Nation:

She

She sounds the Brains of all the young Sotts,
　　That come their to tast her *Elixir;*
Little Flask bottles, and leaking Pint pots,
　　Are framing a fine Coach and six, Sir.

The wanton Virgins frighted: To the last Tune.

YOU that delight in a Jocular Song,
　　Come listen unto me a while, Sir;
I will engage you shall not tarry long,
　　Before it shall make you to smile, Sir:
Near to the Town there liv'd an old Man,
　　Had three pretty Maids to his Daughters;
Of whom I will tell such a story anon.
　　Will tickle your Fancy with Laughter.

The old Man had in his Garden a Pond,
　　'Twas in very fine Summer Weather;
The Daughters one Night they were all very fond,
　　To go and Bath in it together:
Which they agreed, but happen'd to be,
　　O'er heard by a Youth in the House, Sir;
Who got in the Garden, and climb'd up a Tree,
　　And there sate as still as a Mouse, Sir.

The Branch where he sat it hung over the Pond,
　　At each puff of Wind he did totter;
Pleas'd with the Thoughts he should sit abscond,
　　And see them go into the Water:
When the Old Man was safe in his Bed,
　　The Daughters then to the Pond went, Sir;
One to the other two laughing she said,
　　As high as our Bubbies we'll venture.

Upon

Upon the tender green Grass they sat down,
  They all were of delicate Feature ;
Each pluck'd off her Petticoat, Smock, and Gown,
  No sight it could ever be sweeter :
Into the Pond then dabling they went,
  So clean that they needed no Washing ;
But they were all so unluckily bent,
  Like Boys they began to be dashing.

If any body should see us, says one,
  They'd think we were boding of Evil ;
And from the sight of us quickly would run,
  And avoid so many white Devils :
This put the Youth in a merry Pin,
  He let go his hold thro' his Laughter ;
And as it fell out, he fell tumbling in,
  And scar'd them all out of the Water.

The old Man by this time a Noise had heard,
  And rose out of Bed in a Fright, Sir ;
And comes to the Door with a Rusty old Sword,
  There stood in a Posture to fight, Sir :
The Daughters they all came tumbling in,
  And over their Dad they did blunder ;
Who cry'd out aloud, Mercy, good Gentlemen,
  And thought they were Thieves came to Plunder.

The Noise by this time the Neighbours had heard,
  Who came with long Clubs to assist him ;
He told them three bloody Rogues run up Stairs,
  He dar'd by no means to resist them :
For they were Cloathed all in their Buff,
  He see as they shov'd in their Shoulders ;
And black Bandaleers hung before like a ruff,
  Which made them believe they were Soldiers.

The Virgins their Cloaths in the Garden had left,
  And Keys of their Trunks in their Pockets ;
To put on the Sheets they were fain to make shift,
  Their Chest they could not unlock it :

At

At last ventur'd up these Valiant Men,
  Thus armed with Courage undaunted;
But took them for Spirits, and run back again,
  And swore that the House it was Haunted.

As they Retreated the young Man they met,
  Come shivering in at the Door, Sir;
Who look'd like a Rat with his Cloaths dropping wet,
  No Rogue that was Pump'd could look worser:
All were amazed to see him come in,
  And ask'd of him what was the Matter?
He told them the Story, and where he had been,
  Which set them all in a Laughter.

Quoth the old Daddy, I was in a huff,
  And reckon'd to cut them asunder;
Thinking they had been three Soldiers in Buff,
  That came here to rifle and Plunder:
But they are my Daughters whom I loved,
  All Frighted from private Diversion;
Therefore I'll put up my old rusty Sword,
  For why should I be in a Passion.

A *Consolatory* ODE *to Her Majesty.*

ROyal *Flora* dry up your Tears,
　　To cheer the *Allies*, no longer sigh and Mourn ;
Providence blesses your happy Affairs,
　　And resolves for your Loss to make return :
Albion's Trophies flourish each Hour,
　　There Glory by Fame inspir'd gives ravishing sound ;
Flora, whilst *Marcian* disposes her Pow'r,
　　Is the Umpire of Arms, all *Europe* round ;
Thus the *Muse*, tho' ill rewarded and unregarded,
　　　Sings loud with Prophetical hope ;
　　　　Great *Britain's* fears are over,
　　　　We'll soon Recover,
Our dangerous Malady,
Gallia shan't profit by *Ottoman* Unity,
Sweden shall fly before Bears of Cold *Muscovy*,
Spight of Bravadoes of *Orleans*, and *Burgundy*,
　　　Boufflers or *Vendosme*,
　　Or late baffled Troops of the *Pope*.

The PARALLEL : *The Words made to a Tune of Mr.* Eccles's.

THE *Sages* of Old,
  In Prophecy told,
The cause of a Nations undoing ;
  But our new *English* breed,
  No Prophets do need,
For each one here seeks his own Ruin.

  With grumbling and Jarrs,
  We promote Civil Wars,
And Preach up false Tenets too many ;
  We Snarl, and we Bite,
  We Rail, and we Fight
For Religion, yet no man has any.

  Then him let's commend,
  That's true to his Friend,
And the Church, that the Senate does settle ;
  Who delights not in Blood,
  But draws when he shou'd,
And bravely ne'er Shrinks from the Battle.

  Who rails not at Kings,
  Nor at Politick things,
Nor Treason will speak when he's Mellow ;
  But takes a full Glass,
  To King *George's* Success,
This, this is the honest brave fellow.

A BALLAD *of* Andrew *and* Maudlin.

ANdrew and *Maudlin, Rebecca* and *Will,*
  Margaret and *Thomas,* and *Jockey* and *Mary;*
Kate o'th' Kitchin, and *Kit* of the Mill,
  Dick the Plow-man, and *Joan* of the Dairy,
To solace their Lives, and to sweeten their Labour,
All met on a time with a Pipe and Tabor.

Andrew was Cloathed in Shepherd's Grey;
  And *Will* had put on his Holiday Jacket;
Beck had a Coat of *Popin-jay,*
  And *Madge* had a Ribbon hung down to her Placket;
Meg and *Mell* in Frize, *Tom* and *Jockey* in Leather,
And so they began all to Foot it together.

C 2

Their

Their Heads and their Arms about them they flung,
  With all the Might and Force they had ;
Their Legs went like Flays, and as loosely hung,
  They Cudgel'd their Arses as if they were Mad ;
Their Faces did shine, and their Fires did kindle,
While the Maids they did trip and turn like a Spindle.

Andrew chuck'd *Maudlin* under the Chin,
  Simper she did like a Furmity Kettle ;
The twang of whose blubber lips made such a din,
  As if her Chaps had been made of Bell-metal :
Kate Laughed heartily at the same smack,
And loud she did answer it with a Bum-crack.

At no *Whitsun-Ale* there e'er yet had been,
  Such Fraysters and Friskers as these Lads and Lasses;
From their Faces the Sweat ran down to be seen,
  But sure I am, much more from their Arses ;
For had you but seen't, you then would have sworn,
You never beheld the like since you were Born.

Here they did fling, and there they did hoist,
  Here a hot Breath, and there went a Savour ;
Here they did glance, and there they did gloist,
  Here they did Simper, and there they did Slaver ;
Here was a Hand, and their was a Placket,
Whilst, hey ! their Sleeves went Flicket-a-flacket.

The Dance being ended, they Sweat and they Stunk,
  The Maidens did smirk it, the Youngsters did Kiss 'em,
Cakes and Ale flew about, they clapp'd hands and drunk;
  They laugh'd and they gigl'd until they bepist 'em ;
They laid the Girls down, and gave each a green Mantle,
While their Breasts and their Bellies went Pintle a
    Pantle.

A

A SONG, *Sung by a Galley-Slave in* Don Quixote.   *Set by Mr.* Henry Purcell.

W HEN the World first knew creation,
  A Rogue was a top, a Rogue was a top profession;
When there were no more in all Nature but Four,
  There were two of them in Transgression ;
          And the Seeds are no less,
          Since that you may guess,
          But have in all Ages been growing apace ;
          There's Lying, and Thieving,
          Craft, Pride, and Deceiving,
          Rage, Murder, and Roaring,
          Rape, Incest, and Whoring,
Branch out from one Stock, the rank Vices in Vogue.
And make all Mankind one Gygantical Rogue.

          View all human Generation,
          You'll find in every Station,
Lean Vertue decays, whilst Interest sways
          Th' ill Genius of the Nation ;
All are Rogues in Degrees, The Lawyer for Fees,
The Courtier *Leering,* and the Alderman squeez ;
The *Canter,* the Toper, the *Church* Interloper,
The Punk and the *Practice* of *Piety* groper ;
But of all, he that fails our true Rites to maintain,
And deserts the Cause Royal is deepest in grain.

          He that first to mend the matter,
          Made Laws to bind our Nature,
Should have found a way to make Wills obey,
          And have Modell'd new the Creature ;
For the Savage in Man, from Original ran,
And in spight of Confinement now reigns as't began ;
Here's Preaching and Praying, and Reason displaying,
Yet Brother with Brother, is Killing and Slaying ;
Then blame not the Rogue that free Sense does enjoy,
Then falls like a Log, and believes he shall lye.

Pretty

Pretty KATE *of* Windsor: *A new* BALLAD.

NEar to the Town of *Windsor,* upon a pleasant
      Green,
  There liv'd a Miller's Daughter, her Age about
      Eighteen.
A Skin as white as Alablaster, and a killing Eye,
A round Plump bonny Buttock joyn'd to a taper Thigh;
  Then ah! be kind, my Dear, be kinder, was the Ditty still,
  When pretty Kate *of* Windsor *came to the Mill.*

To treat with her in Private, first came a Booby Squire,
He offer'd ten broad Pieces, but she refus'd the hire;
She said his Corn was musty, nor should her Toll-dish
      fill,
His Measure too so scanty, she fear'd 'twould burn her
      Mill.   *Then ah! be kind, &c.*

Soon after came a Lawyer, as he the Circuit went,
He swore he'd Cheat her Landlord, and she should pay
      no Rent;
He question'd the Fee simple; but him she plainly
      told,
I'll keep in spight of Law Tricks, mine own dear Copy-
      hold.   *Then ah! be kind, &c.*

The next came on a Trooper, that did of Fighting prate,
Till she pull'd out his Pistol, and knock'd him o're the
      Pate.
I hate, she cry'd, a Hector, a Drone without a Sting,
For if you must be Fighting Friend, go do it for the
      King.   *Then ah! be kind, &c.*

A late discarded Courtier, would next her favour win,
He offer'd her a Thousand when e'er King *James* came in;
She laugh'd at that extreamly, and said it was too small,
For if he e'er comes in again, you'll get the Devil and all.
  Then ah! be kind, &c.

Next came a strutting Sailor that was of Mates degree,
He bragg'd much of his Valour in the late Fight at Sea;

She told him his Bravado's but lamely did appear,
For if you had stood to't, you Rogues, the *French* had
    ne'er came here.   *Then ah ! be kind,* &c.

A Shopkeeper of *London* then open'd his Love Case,
He told her he was Famous for Penning an Address ;
She told City-wisdom was known by their Affairs,
Guild-Hall was full of Wit too in choice of Sheriffs
    and Mayors.
    Then ah ! be kind, &c.

Next came a smug Physician upon a Pacing Mare,
But she declar'd she lik'd him much worse than any
    there ;
He was so us'd to Glisters, she told him to his Face,
He always would be bobbing his Pipe at the wrong
    place.
    Then ah ! be kind, &c.

The Parson of the Town then did next his flame
    reveal,
She made him second Mourning, and cover'd him
    with Meal ;
The Man of God stood fretting, she bid him not be
    vext,
'Twill serve you for a Surplice to Cant in *Sunday* next.
    Then ah ! be kind, &c.

Now if you'd know the reason she was to them
    unkind,
There was a brisk young Farmer that taught her still
    to grind ;
She knew him for a Workman that had the ready
    skill,
To open well her Water-gate, and best supply her
    Mill.
    *Then ah ! be kind, my Dear, be kinder, was the
       Ditty still,*
    When pretty Kate *of* Windsor *came to the Mill.*
                        Tom

TOM *and* DOLL.
Or, the Modest Maid's Delight.

When

WHen the Kine had giv'n a Pail full,
    And the Sheep came bleating home ;
Doll who knew it would be healthful,
    Went a walking with young *Tom :*
        Hand in hand Sir,
        O're the Land Sir,
As they walked to and fro ;
    Tom made jolly Love to *Dolly*,
But was answer'd, *No, no, no, no, no,* &c.

Faith, says *Tom*, the time is fitting,
    We shall never get the like ;
You can never get from Knitting,
    Whilst I'm digging in the Dike :
        Now we're gone too,
        And alone too,
No one by to see or know ;
    Come, come, *Dolly*, prithee shall I ?
Still she answer'd, *No, no, no, no,* &c.

Fie upon you Men, quoth *Dolly*,
    In what snares you'd make us fall ;
You'll get nothing but the folly,
    But I shall get the Devil and all :
        Tom with sobs,
        And some dry Bobs,
Cry'd *you're a fool to argue so ;*
    Come, come, *Dolly*, shall I ? shall I ?
Still she answer'd *No, no, no, no,* &c.

To the Tavern then he took her,
    Wine to *Love's* a Friend confest
By the hand he often shook her,
    And drank brimmers to the best, *&c.*
        Doll grew warm,
        And thought no harm ;
Till after a brisk pint or two,
    To what he said the silly Maid,
Could hardly bring out, *No, no, no, no,* &c.

She

She swore he was the prettiest Fellow
  In the Country or the Town,
And began to grow so mellow,
  On the Couch he laid her down ;
      Tom came to her,
      For to woe her
Thinking this the time to try :
  Something past so kind at last,
Her no was chang'd to *I, I, I, I, I, I,* &c.

Closely then they joyn'd their Faces,
  Lovers you know what I mean ;
Nor could she hinder his Embraces,
  Love was now too far got in ;
      Both now lying,
      Panting dying,
Calms succeed the stormy Joy,
  Tom wou'd fain renew't again,
And she consents with I, I, I, I, I, I, *&c.*

The Lovers' Whims.   A New Song.

WHen I make a fond Address,
    Then *Phillis* seems cruel ;
Tho' I talk of sad Distress,
Yet she still frowns ;
But the coyness that she shews,
Increases my Fewel.
What in others stops repose,
My Delight crowns :
When she makes the house Ring,
Then a Bottle I bring ;
And if her Voice is,
Swell'd with Noises,
Tope my glass and Sing.

Ever have I lov'd a Lass
Of *Phillis's* Humour ;
Let her Scold and Screw her Face
Twenty Thousand ways,
With the Frolicks I return,
I'le always o'recome her,
And the more she seems to Scorn,
Me the more she'll please .
Take the softly she,
Tamely then agree,
The Spritely speaking,
Not the sneaking,
Is the Lass for me.

A Scotch Song, *sung to the King at* Windsor.

J Ust when the young and blooming Spring
　　Had melted down the Winter Snow ;
And in the Grove the Birds did Sing,
　　Their charming Notes on ev'ry Bough :
Poor *Willy* sate bemoaning his fate,
　　And woful state,
For loving, loving, loving,
　　And despairing too ;
Alas ! he'd cry, that I must dye,
　　For pretty *Kate* of *Edenbrough.*

Willy was late at a Wedding house,
　　Where Lords and Ladies danc'd all arow ;
But *Willy* saw nene so pretty a Lass,
　　As pretty *Kate* of *Edenbrough.*
Her bright Eyes, with smiling Joys,
　　Did so surprise ;
And something, something, something
　　Else that shot him through :
Thus *Willy* lies entranc'd in Joys,
　　With pretty *Kate* of *Edenbrough.*

The God of Love was *Willy's* friend,
　　And cast an Eye of Pity down ;
And straight a fatal Dart did send,
　　The cruel Virgin's Heart to wound.
Now every Dream is all of him,
　　Who still does seem
More lovely, lovely, lovely,
　　Since the Marriage Vow :
Thus *Willy* lies entranc'd in Joys,
　　With pretty *Kate* of *Edenbrough.*

The

The JILTS; *a* SONG.

Sung to the KING at Winchester.

ON a Bank in flowry *June,*
    When Groves are green and gay;
In a smiling Afternoon,
    With *Doll* young *Willy* lay:
They thought none were to spy 'em,
But *Nell* stood list'ning by 'em;

                                        Oh

Oh fye ! *Doll* cry'd, no, I vow, I'de rather dye ;
Than wrong my Modesty :
Quoth *Nell*, that I shall see.

Smarting pain the Virgin finds,
　　Although by Nature taught,
When she first to Man inclines ;
　　Quoth *Nell* I'll venture that.
Then who would loose a Treasure
For such a puney Pleasure?
　　Not I, not I, no, a Maid I'll live and dye,
And to my Vow be true :
Quoth *Nell*, the more fool you.

To my Closet I'll repair,
　　And Godly Books peruse ;
Then devote my self to Pray'r,
　　Quoth *Nell*, and ―― use ;
You Men are all perfidious,
But I will be Religious.
　　Try all, fly all, whil'st I have Breath deny ye all,
For the Sex I now despise :
Quoth *Nell*, by G—d she lies.

Youthful Blood o'respreads her Face,
　　When Nature prompts to Sin :
Modesty ebbs out apace,
　　And Love as fast flows in :
The Swain that heard this schooling,
Asham'd, left off his fooling ;
　　Kill me, kill me, now I am ruin'd, let me dye :
You have damn'd my Soul to Hell ;
Try her once again, cries *Nell.*

To SYLVIA.

A SONG *set to a New Playhouse Tune.*

S Tate and Ambition, alas ! will deceive ye,
    There's no solid Joy but the Blessing of Love ;
Scorn does of Pleasure fair *Sylvia* bereave ye,
    Your Fame is not perfect till that you remove :
Monarchs that sway the vast Globe in their Glory,
    Know Love is their brightest Jewel of Pow'r ;
Poor *Philemon's* Heart was ordain'd to adore ye,
    Ah ! then disdain his Passion no more.

Jove on his Throne was the Victim of Beauty,
    His thunder laid by, he from Heaven came down ;
Shap'd like a Swan, to fair *Leda* paid Duty,
    And priz'd her far more than his Heav'nly crown :
She too was pleas'd with her beautiful Lover,
    And stroak'd his white Plums, and feasted her Eye ;
His cunning in Loving knew well how to move her,
    By Billing begins the business of Joy.

Since Divine Powers Examples have given,
    If we should not follow their Precepts, we sin :
Sure 'twill appear an Affront to their Heaven,
    If when the Gate opens we enter not in.
Beauty my Dearest was from the beginning,
    Created to calm our Amorous Rage ;
And she that against that Decree will be sinning,
    In Youth still will find the Curse of old Age.

The PERFECTION,

A New SONG.   *To the Dutchess of* Grafton.
Set to Musick by Dr. John Blow.

WE all to conqu'ring Beauty bow,
  Its pleasing Pow'r admire ;
But I ne'er knew a Face 'till now,
  That like yours could inspire.
Now I may say, I met with one,
  Amazes all Mankind ;
And like Men gazing on the Sun,
  With too much light am blind.

Soft as the tender moving Sighs,
  When longing Lovers meet ;
Like the dividing Prophets wise,
  And like blown Roses sweet :
Modest, yet Gay ; Reserv'd, yet Free ;
  Each happy Night a Bride ;
A Mein like awful Majesty,
  And yet no spark of Pride.

The Patriarch, to gain a Wife,
  Chast, Beautiful, and Young :
Serv'd fourteen Years a painful Life,
  And never thought 'em long.
Ah ! were you to reward such Cares,
  And Life so long couldst stay ;
Not fourteen, but four hundred Years,
  Would seem but as one Day.

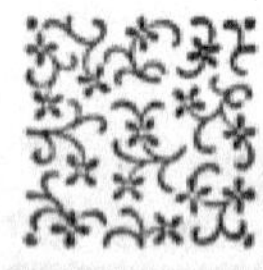

The DISTRUST.

A New Song, *set to Musick by*
Mr. John Lenton.

NO, silly *Cloris !*
    Tell me no such Stories,
True gen'rous Love can never undo ye ;
    When I desert ye,
    Let affected Virtue,
Charm ev'ry Fop that now does pursue ye :
    Search all human Nature,
    Try ev'ry Creature,
Study all Complexions,
    Ev'ry Face and Feature ;
    And when e're I dye,
    You'll too late descry,
None ever yet did Love so well as I.

    Curse on Ambition,
    What a bless'd condition
Lovers were in, not aw'd by that *Dæmon;*
    Then cruel *Cloris !*
    Careless of Vain-Glories,
Would reap more Bliss than Pride e'er could dream on :
    We should have no dying,
    No Self-denying,
Sighings or Repulses,
    When the Soul is flying ;
    But truly wise,
    Dirt she would despise,
And own her Love the Crown of all her Joys.

The

The PASSION.

Set to Musick by Mr. Samuel Akeroyd.

BY all the Pow'rs! I love you so,
   Nothing's so dear to me below;
And when I would your scorn forsake,
Some Angel turns, and brings me back:
   Altho' my Heart's not fool'd with ease,
Yet you may break it when you please;
   'Tis noble, and does rather dare to dye,
Than languish and despair.

Ah! tell me not that Men deceive,
But if you'd be believ'd, believe;
My Heart, like Tapers shut in Urns,
Whilst Love gives matter ever burns:
   Since kindness has resistless Charms,
And Beauty, wanting Youth, decays;
   Make hast, and fly into my Arms,
And crown my bless'd remaining Days.

Joy *after* Sorrow.

A New SONG.   *The Words made to the Duke* D'Aumonds *Minuet.*

L ET *Burgundy* flow,
    Let the Glass run o'er, let the Glass run o'er
        boys,
    To cure all our Woe,
Let the Glass run over the Brim,
    Though *Anna* is gone,
Think of it no more, think of it no more boys,
    Great *George* now comes on,
Toast away your Bumpers to him,
        Tho' the Feuds were so big
        'Twixt the *Tory* and *Whigg*,
That the Mischiefs pursuing prov'd almost our Ruin,
        Like a Prophet I know,
        They will be no more so,
We've a King will unite now both *High-Church* and *Low.*

        And now your Hand's in
Fill it up again, fill it up again there,
        To all these brave Men,
Who their Hate to *Lorrain* bear strong,
        Who frentick with Pride
Boldly durst defend, lately the *Pretender*,
        And if I'm not wide,
Will be sure to pay for't e'er long,
        Nor a less Glass let's have
        To the *Catalans* brave,
Who held out with a Glory, not equall'd in Story,
        For not *Cæsar* in *Gaul*,
        Nor the great *Hannibal*,
Ever equall'd their Chief, with a number so small.

A

A Song, *sung in my Play of the Campaigners,*
extreamly divertive, just after Mr. ———
C———t's *vile Satyr upon Poets and the Stage.*
Set to a Tune of Mr. Henry Purcell's.

NEW Reformation begins thro' the Nation,
    And our grumbling Sages, that hope for good wages,
        Direct us the way :
Sons of the Muses, then cloak your Abuses,
And least you shou'd trample on pious Example,
        Observe and obey.
Time frenzy Curers, and stubborn *Nonjurors,*
For want of Diversion, now scourge the leud Times :
They've hinted, they've printed, our vein it profane is,
        And worst of all Crimes ;
Dull clod pated Railers, Smiths, Coblers and Colliers,
        Have damn'd all our Rhimes.

Under the Notion of Zeal for Devotion,
The Humour has fir'd em, or rather inspir'd 'em,
        To tutor the Age :
But if in Season, you'd know the true Reason ;
The hopes of Preferment, is what make the Vermin,
        Now rail at the Stage.
Cuckolds and Canters, with Scruples and Banters ;
The Old Forty-one Peal, against Poetry ring :
But let State Revolvers, and Treason Absolvers,
        Excuse me if I sing,
The Rebel that chuses to cry down the Muses,
Wou'd cry down the King.

Gillian *of* Croyden, *a New* Ballad: *The Words made to the Tune of a Country Dance, call'd* Mall Peatly.

ONE Holiday last Summer,
  From four to seven by *Croyden Chimes*,
Three Lasses toping Rummers,
  Were set a prating of the Times,
    A Wife call'd *Joan* of the Mill,
    A Maid they call'd bonny brown *Nell*,
A Widow mine Hostess *Gillian* of *Croyden*, *Gillian* of
Croyden, *Gillian*, young *Gillian*, *Jolly Gillian* of *Croyden*,
Take off your Glass, cry'd *Gillian* of *Croyden*,
    A Health to our Master *Will*.

Ah! *Joan*, cry'd the Maiden,
  This Peace will bring in Mill'd Money store,
We now shan't miss of Trading,
  And Sweet-hearts will come on thick ye Whore :
    No more will they fight and kill,
    But with us good Liquor will swill :
These will be rare Times, cry'd *Gillian* of *Croyden*,
Gillian of *Croyden*, *Gillian*, young *Gillian*, plump
Gillian of *Croyden*, take off your Glass, cry'd *Gillian*
    of *Croyden*,
    A Bumper to Master *Will*.

We've now right Understanding,
  Hans, *Dick*, and *Mounsieur* shakes Hands i'th' Streets,
Dragoons too are disbanding,
  Gadzooks, then *Nelly* let's watch our Sheets,
    For a Red-coat you know that has Will,
    Can plunder and pilfer with Skill ;
I'll look to my Smocks, cry'd *Gillian* of *Croyden*,
Gillian of Croyden, *Gillian*, bold *Gillian*, wary *Gillian* of
Croyden, take off your Glass, cry'd *Gillian* of *Croyden*,
    A Health to our Master *Will*.

Nell, then with Arms a-Kembo,
  Cry'd News from Sea not so well does come ;
For want of Captain *Bembo*,
  The Chink and *Ponti* are safe got home :

Tho'

Tho' he could not help that Ill,
The Fault lies in some Body still,
Wou'd that Rogue were hang'd, cry'd *Gillian* of *Croyden,*
Gillian of *Croyden, Gillian,* plump *Gil.,* Loyal *Gil.* &c.

Strange Lords will now come over,
And all our Bells will ring out for Joy :
The Czar of *Muscover*
Who is, Lord bless him, some ten Foot high :
I'll see whate'er comes o'th' Mill,
Wou'd our Lads were like him, cry'd *Nell,*
Great pity they an't, cry'd *Gillian* of *Croyden, Gillian* of
Croyden, Gillian, young *Gillian,* Tall *Gillian* of *Croyden,*
Nevertheless, cry'd *Gillian* of *Croyden,*
A Bumper to Master *Will.*

Strange News, the *Jacks* of the City
Have got, cry'd *Joan,* but we mind no Tales ;
That our good King thro' wonderful Pity,
Will give his Crown to the Prince of *Wales,*
That Peace may the stronger be still,
And that they may no longer rebel,
Pish! pox tis a Jest, cry'd *Gillian* of *Croyden, Gillian* of
Croyden, Gillian, bold *Gillian,* witty *Gillian* of *Croyden,*
Take off your Glass, cry'd *Gillian* of *Croyden,*
A Health to our Master *Will.*

So long top'd these Lasses,
Till Tables, Chairs, and Stools went round,
Strong Wine, and thumping Glasses,
In three short Hours their Senses drown'd :
Then home to her Grannum reel'd *Nell,*
And *Joan* no more Brimmers could fill,
And off from her Chair drop'd *Gillian* of *Croyden, Gillian*
Of *Croyden, Gillian,* plump *Gillian,* drunk *Gillian* of
Croyden, here's the last drop, cry'd *Gillian* of *Croyden,*
A Bumper to Master *Will.*

A

A SONG *to* CELIA, *who was forc'd to Marry another, her Lover being absent: Made to the Amiable* Vanqure.

AH, tell me no more of your Duty or Vow,
That Change of Condition no Love can allow;
    I still must Importune,
    For what my curst Fortune,
    Lost I know not how!
And since such ill chances have often been Common,
  That Wealth or Women we're fated to lose;
  'Tis fit we our selves should mend such abuse;
    And make with our fetters,
    The best of bad matters;
    In Wedlocks Trappan,
    By taking occasion,
    To ease our wrong'd Passion
    As well as we can.

NEW-

NEWMARKET:

A SONG, *sung to the King there.*

THE

THE Golden Age is come,
　　The Winter Storms are gone ;
Flowers spread and bloom,
　And smile to see the Sun :

Who daily gilds the Groves,
　And calms the Air and Seas ;
Nature seems in love,
　When all the World's in peace.

Ye Rogues go saddle *Ball*,
　I'le to *Newmarket* scour ;
You never mind when I call,
　You should have been ready this hour :

For there are the Sports and the Games,
　Without any plotting of State ;
From Treason, or any such shame,
　Deliver us, deliver us, Oh Fate !

Let's be to each other a Prey,
　To be cheated be ev'ry ones lot ;
Or chows'd any sort of way,
　But by another Plot.

Let Cullies that lose at a Race,
　Go venture at Hazard and win ;
And he that is bubbled at Dice,
　Recover it at Cocking again.

Let Jades that are founder'd be bought,
　Let Jockeys play Crimp to make sport ;
For faith it was strange methought,
　To see *Tinker* beat the Court.

Each corner of the Town
　Rings with perpetual noise,
The Oyster-bawling Clown
　Joyns with Hot Pudding-pies :

Who

Who both in Consort keep,
  To vend their stinking Ware ;
The drowzy God of Sleep,
  Has no Dominion here.

Hey-boys, the Jockeys roar,
  If the Mare and Gelding run ;
I'll hold ye five Guineas to four,
  He'll beat her and give half a Stone.

Gad Dam-me cries Bully, 'tis done,
  Or else I'm the Son of a Whore ;
And would I could meet with a Man
  Will offer it, will offer it once more.

See, see the damn'd Vice of this Town,
  A Fop that was starving of late,
And scarcely could borrow a Crown,
  Puts in to run for the Plate.

Another makes Racing a Trade,
  And dreams of his Projects to come ;
And many a crimp Match has made,
  By bubbing another Man's Groom.

The Townsmen are Whiggish, God rot 'em,
  Their Hearts are but Loyal by fits ;
For if we should search to the bottom,
  They're nasty as their Streets.

But now all Hearts beware,
  See, see on yonder Downs,
Beauty triumphs there,
  And at this distance wounds.

In the *Amazonian* Wars,
  Thus all the Virgins shone ;
Thus like glittering Stars,
  Paid Homage to the Moon.

Love

Love proves a Tyrant now,
  And here does proudly dwell ;
For each stubborn Spirit must bow,
  He has found out a new way to kill :

For ne'er was invented before,
  Such Charms of additional Grace ;
Nor had Divine Beauty such Power,
  In every, in every fair Face.

Udsbows, cries my Country-man *John*,
  Was ever the like before seen ?
By Hats and the Feathers they'd on
  I took 'em all for Men :

Embroider'd and fine as the Sun,
  On Horses in Trappings of Gold,
Such a Show I shall ne'er see again,
  Should I live to a hundred years old.

This, this, is the Country Discourse,
  All wond'ring at the rare sight,
'Then *Roger* go saddle my Horse,
  For I will be there to night.

Love

Love Unblinded.

A New Song, *set to Musick by Mr.* William Turner.

MY Life and my Death were once in your pow'r,
I languish'd each moment, and dy'd ev'ry hour ;
But now your ill usage has open'd my Eyes,
I can free my poor Heart, and give others Advice :
By Dissembling and Lies the Coquet may be won,
But he that loves faithfully will be undone.

Time was, false *Aurelia*, I thought you as bright
As Angels adorn'd in the Glories of Light ;
But your Pride and Ingratitude now, I thank Fate,
Have taught my dull Sence to distinguish the Cheat :
And now I can see in your face no such Prize,
No Charms in your Person, no Darts in your Eyes.

Fain, fain for your sake my Amours I would end,
And the rest of my days give my Books, and my Friend ;
But another kind Fair calls me fool, to destroy,
For the sake of one Jilt, my whole Life's greatest Joy :
For tho' Friends, Wine, and Books, make Life's Dia-
dem shine,
Love, Love is the Jewel that makes it so fine.

The STORM:

Set to Musick by Mr. Henry Purcell.

CHORUS.

Farewel

Farewell ye Rocks, ye Seas, and Sands,
  Green *Neptune* I despise ;
I'll rather court the pleasant Strands,
  Then all his watry Joys :
Inconstant Bliss our Fate beguiles,
  The Sea like Love we find ;
Where Calms are like fair *Cynthia's* Smiles,
  And frowns like gusts of Wind.

C H O R U S.

Hear the noise of the Tarpawlian Boys;
    Port, Port, Port,
Luff hawl aft the Sheet is the Mariner's Wit :
A plague of their ignorant Prattle,
  And send me to land, and send me to land,
      Where I may command,
A pretty kind Wench,
  A pretty kind Wench, and a Bottle.

With all God's Miracles at Land
  Let me acquainted be ;
Let Fools that would understand,
  Go find them out at Sea.
His mighty Works I'll praise on Shore,
  And there his Blessings reap ;
But from this moment seek no more,
  His Wonders in the Deep.

CHO. *Port, Port,* &c.

The Merchant, when his Sails are furl'd,
  Glides o're the foamy Main ;
And ploughs with ease the watry World,
  So great a Charm is Gain :
When Avarice has any Bounds,
  If his contented were ;
I'd wage a hundred thousand Pounds,
  He never would come there.

CHO. *Port, Port,* &c.

A

A Dialogue betwixt ALEXIS *and* SYLVIA :

Set to Musick by Mr. Henry Purcell.

Alexis. SIt down my dear *Sylvia,*
  And then tell me, tell me true,
When we the fierce pleasure of Passion first
  knew ;
What Senses were charm'd,
And what Raptures did dwell,
Within thy fond Heart, my dear Nymph,
  prithee tell !
That when thy Delights in their fulness are known,
I may have the joy to relate all my own.

Sylvia. Oh fye, my *Alexis !*
  How dare you propose,
To me silly Girl, things immodest as those !
Nice Candor and Modesty glow in my Breast,
Whose Virtue can utter no Words so unchast ;
But if your impatience admits no delay,
Describe your own Raptures,
And teach me the way.

Alexis. A pain mix'd with Pleasure my Senses first
  found,
When crouds of Delight strait my Heart did
  surround ;
A Joy so transporting, I sigh'd when it was done :
And fain would renew, but alas ! all was gone :
Coy nature was treacherous, when first she ment,
A Treasure so precious so soon should be spent.

Sylvia. This free kind Confession does so much prevail,
  That I in your bosom would blush out my Tale ;
  But Dearest, you know, 'tis too much to declare,
  The Joys that our Souls, when united, do share.
Let this then suffice, if the Pleasure could last,
A Saint would leave Heav'n, still so to be blest.

On

On AUGUSTUS *and* SOPHRONIA :

Set to Musick by Senior Baptist.   *On King*
Charles *the* II*d. and the Dutchess of* ———

A *Ugustus* crown'd with Majesty,
   His weighty Cares removing ;
Beheld his World, but nought could spye,
   Worth Royal Thought but Loving :
A Synod of the Gods appear,
   And vote their Sacred Sence ;
That none but the divinest Fair,
   Should bless the greatest Prince.

So

Sophronia their Command obeys,
  Sophronia their chief Blessing ;
With Dove-like Innocence, her Face
  Was sweet beyond expressing :
A Time commanding Beauty must,
  While the World lasts, be fine ;
And when the World is shook to dust,
  The Sun will cease to shine.

The Coquet *New Moulded: A New* Song.

Ho' *Cælia* Art you shew,
    It must not pass upon me now ;
The bright Smiles grace your Brow,
Deceit has Gilded o'er
Your soft Words, when I wooe,
To prove your Love is firm and true,
Depend on't never shall do,
Unless you grant me more :

You

You, Sharper-like, shew Wit,
And cunningly all my Coyn you get,
Throw false Dice when I Sett,
And never play me fair ;
But now to overreach you,
By a subtle care,
I am resolv'd to teach you,
To Play upon the Square.

You Sing, Dance, finely you Play,
A thousand Pretty Things you say ;
And then in niggardly way,
You give a Lenten Treat :
The cold Tast favours your wish,
And oft you highly praise the Dish ;
But I have hatred to fish,
My Stomach craves some Meat.

Leave this Coquettish blind,
The Subtlety of your Serpent kind ;
Plain dealing let me find,
Attoning for late mishaps :
My hungry Love in quiet,
Can't be with Cordial Drops ;
It wants substantial Dyet,
And cannot feed on Scraps.

The Church Jockey, *a Comick* S A T Y R.   *The*
Words made to a pretty Play-house Tune.

THE Parliament sate
　　　As snug as a Cat ;
In Old loyal Brome you may read,
　　　And ours in their House,
　　　Were as close as a Mouse,
Legislating the Nation with Speed.

　　　Peace sounded by Fame,
　　　Whether true, or a Shame,
Still puzzled the People to know ;
　　　But the Lottery went right,
　　　Which some thought a Bite,
Tho' the Money at last came but slow.

　　　The Price of Corn fell,
　　　And all Matters look'd well,
For none State Proceedings could blame,
　　　When a hot headed Priest
　　　Gave a plaguy Distast,
That has put all the Town in a flame.

　　　Whose raving uncouth,
　　　Even foaming at Mouth
Was Interest, as each one believes ;
　　　Not a jot of true Zeal
　　　For the good Common-weal,
But to get a good pair of lawn Sleeves.

　　　St. *Peter* and *Paul*
　　　Gave with mildness a Call,
To such as they found wanted Grace ;
　　　But our *Rabbi* Lords,
　　　If you won't take their Words,
Like the Furies, shall fly in your Face.

　　　A-duce take their Chat,
　　　Can't they eat and grow fat,
We know well their Stripends are large,
　　　But with jangling debates
　　　They must plague three Estates,
Besides putting the Queen to such Charge.

Yet

Yet this the New Case
Of our Soul-mender was
Who rank in the *Tory* Affair ;
With his Tongue did so charm,
(Heav'n keep us from Harm)
He was like to draw in my Lord M———r.

But my Lord having Grace,
As you see in his Face,
Did strait to uphold him refuse,
And at last being own'd,
As a member renown'd
Made a shift to slip out of the Noose.

In the good days of old,
When the Doctrine worth Gold,
Do devout Congregations oblige ;
The Priest honour gain'd,
If i'th' Church he might stand,
But now they will ride on the Ridge.

Like Jockeys they whirr,
With a whip and a Spurr,
That ambitious designs mayn't be crost ;
Tho' by running at all,
They oft lose by a fall,
Or by blundring the wrong side the Post.

Ye Elders in black,
Sober counsel pray take,
Cease railing, for which y'are so fam'd ;
For if that be your way,
You may Preach, you may pray,
If the Wise ever heed, I'll be D———d.

For if they teach right,
Jarring minds to unite,
And Angel-like, that man is blest ;
The contrary's good,
That who stirs them to feud,
The Devil must be of a Priest.

The

The Country SHEEP-SHEARING: *Made to the Watermens Dance.*

J Enney and *Molly*, and *Dolly*,
  When young Lambs were a Roaring;
  Robin and *Willey*, and *Harry*,
  Met all at a Sheep-Shearing:

Lately

Lately a Match was made,
Plump *Jone* of the Valley,
Simper'd till Grace was said,
With *Roger* the Jolly:
Hodg the brisk and strong,
Could well give her a Fairing;
Joan the fresh and Young,
The best at the Sheep-Shearing.

Kissing and Pressing, the Blessing
Went round, none did resist 'em;
Sherry, brown Berry and Perry,
They drank till they bepist 'em:
Phillip some Fish had brought,
That newly were taken,
Kitt too had Coleworts bought,
For *Barnabys* Bacon.
Curds and Cream Divine,
The kind Lasses indearing,
Never Feast so fine,
Was known at a Sheep-shearing:

But whilst they trolling down derry,
Were all Eating and Drinking;
Never were Creatures so merry,
Faith, to e'ry ones thinking;
Georgy came Jumping in,
Without any bidding,
He had a Rival been,
And swore at the Wedding,
Cuffs and Kicks went round,
No speaking or hearing,
Thus in brawl was drown'd
Our Jolly Sheep-shearing.

An ODE, *On the* King's *happy Return from abroad: To a Sebell of Mr.* Henry Purcell's.

Crown your Bowls Loyal souls,
  Cæsar to his Home returns ;
From the Shore, Cannons roar,
  England Smiles and *Holland* mourns :
Malecontents in Mischief failing,
Changing notes now leave off railing ;
Now the Vipers hide their stings,
  Fill, fill then high, proclaim, proclaim your joy ;
And now in a Chorus sing, welcome best of Kings,
  Noble Boys here's to thee,
  Look on my Glass and me,
    Here's the way,
    We this happy day,
Make as fam'd as the *Jubilee.*
Make as fam'd as the *Jubilee.*

LEWIS

LEWIS *upon the fret ; A Satyrical* ODE, *upon the* French *King's huffing Threat on the* English *Addresses: With some Remarks upon his Character.*

L *Ewis le* Grand,
    With Coquet *Maintenon,*
Upon a Bed of State were laid along,
    One Hand around,
    About his Neck was thrown,
The tother gently scratching his bald Crown ;
    London's News
    Just then perus'd,
He cry'd, *Le Diable,* was e'er seen such dam Abuse ;
    Dat *Papier dere*
    From *Angleterre,*
    Foulieu Addresse,
    Dat croud the Presse,
Begar make me de monster worst of Jews.

    My Old Trick,
    And noted Politick,
Dat what I vow and swear am sure to break ;
    Though 'tis true,
    Vat have de Mob to do,
Avec les Rois, and State Affaire *Morbleau ;*
    Laws me take,
    Or else forsake,
Comme proprement le fine of my Designs dey make ;
    Dam gilling Whore,
    Et Louis d'or
    Dat bubl'd le langue
    Des Parliament,
Jernie make two Fool of late King *Charle* and *Jaque.*

    Charle and de Queen,
    Louis and *Mazarine,*
Still play'd de Game where I was sure to win,
    He feed de Ducks,
    And speak de merry Jokes,
Whilst I was building Ships with *English* Oakes ;
                                    Jaque

Jaque dat reign'd,
De next I gain'd,
Bougre my shaven Crowns his Purse and Senses drain'd,
"Till like a Sot,
I turn'd Bigot,
And for de Fault
Away must trot,
Since when de whole Brood begar me have maintain'd.

Now mark de Jest,
Old *Jaque* is gone to rest,
And I have make de King of my Welch Guest,
Tho' some dat speak
Of dat *Italian* Trick
Will swear his true Papa did make de Brick ;
Be't what 'twill,
Good or Ill,
Morbleu, dis is de way for him to pay my Bill :
And now dey rore,
Like Son of Whore,
And make Address
Dat scratch my Face,
Me will chastise 'em, *Morbleu*, me will.

Scarce had de Boast
From *France* come over Post,
When he de *Blenheim* Field to *Marlborough* lost,
And soon again,
Rammille and *Turin*,
With Victory conclude de glorious Campaign,
Whish sad Blow
Perplex'd him so,
I cry'd, Jilt Fortune now is turn'd my Foe,
Marsin is dead,
Bavarre is fled,
(Here *Maintenon*)
Vat must be done,
Me sal be L'Emperour le *Diable* know when.

PILLS *to Purge Melancholy.*

The Franck LOVER; *a New* SONG.

DEarest believe without a Reservation,
  What neither Time nor Fate shall e'er controul;
Be you but kind and constant to your Passion,
  No stormy chance shall e'er disturb my Soul;
Jealousie, the bane to Lovers pleasures,
  Far from our Hearts for ever we'll remove;
My full Joy, what Mortal then can measure,
  Happy in my charming *Musidora's* Love.

When with a Friend abroad I take a Bottle,
  Over your *Tea* regale with who you can;
Or if you find me with a Vizard prattle,
  Do you the same with any other Man;
For *Chloe's* Face when Ogling I shew Passion,
  'Tis all but feign'd, I can ne'er inconstant be;
And when at large I tope the red Potation,
  'Twill but more inflame my Heart with Love of thee.

The

The National Quarrel ; a New BALLAD.

Shone

SHone a *Welch* Runt, and *Hans* a *Dutch* Boor,
　As they one Ev'ning for Air did employ;
Found *Teague* and *Sawney* just walking before,
　A bonny *Scotch* Loon, and an *Irish* dear Joy:
They all four ne'er saw a Windmill,
　Nor had they heard of any such Name;
But as they were walking, and merrily talking,
　It happen'd by chance to a Windmill they came.

The Chorus goes to the last Part of the Tune.

　　Hey down derry, hoa down derry,
　　　Mirth is better than Sorrow by half;
　　Listen to my Ditty, 'tis merry, 'tis Witty,
　　　And if ye an't Sullen 'twill make ye Laugh.

Bread, cry'd *Sawney*, what do ye caw * that?
　To tell its good Name I am at a loss;
Teague then readily answer'd the *Scot*,
　By Creesht, my dear Joy, 'tis St. *Patrick's* Cross:
Woons, cry'd *Sawney*, y'are mistaken,
　For 'tis St. *Andrew's* Cross that I swear;
For there is his Bonnet, and Plad lying on it,
　The muckle gud Saint did at *Edinborough* wear.
　　Sawney, Sawney, *weel said* Sawney,
　　　This Affair Sawney *notably hit;*
　　Let aw discover that pass the Tweed *over,*
　　　If Scotland *e're bred so bonny a Wit.*

Hans with a Belch gave vent in his turn,
　† *Ick sall now spraeken den vaght it dos* mean;
et ben ods Sacrament a grought *Dutch* Churne,
　And they are now making the Butter within:
This device so tickled his fancy,
　He swore by the *States* he'd go in for some;
And sell his blue Jerkin, but he'd have a Firkin,
　To carry his Wife and his Family home.

---

* *Pointing to the Windmill.*　　† *Mimicks* Dutch.
Hogan

Hogan, Hogan, Mogan, Mogan,
   Sooterkin Hogan, Herring Vandunck ;
For as it happen'd the Miller with's Cap on,
   He thought a fat Froe, a white Dairy Punk.

Hot pated *Shone* cry'd splut and look'd pig,
   You fools was alter your minds when hur speaks ;
St. *Taffy* cawd this her crete Whirligig,
   And made it to scare away Crows from her Leeks,
Proof to shew, see where they Grow,
   Then pointed his Finger over the hedge,
Where Nettles and Thistles, with Prickles and Bristles,
   Grew thick in a field grown over with sedge.
     Shone ap Shinkin Rice ap Tavy,
       Shentlemen Kindred aw come away ;
     Tomas *ap* Morgan *swear loud as an Organ,*
       And pawn all your Honours to what hur does say.

By good St. *Patrick, Teague* once more replies,
   I say 'tis his Cross, for there is his Coat ;
I met him in *Dublin* a buying the Frize,
   And gud I will swear, 'tis the same that he bought :
He's a better Shaint than ever *Holland,* or *Walsh,* or
   Scotland, can breed,
   And by my Showlwasion he was my Relation,
And had for stout *Teague* great kindness indeed.
     Lero, lero, lero, lero,
       Lilly Burlero Bullen a-la ;
     By my Showlwasion he was my Relation,
       Chreesht save thy sweet Face St. Patrick Agra.

Each gave his mind, but neither agreed,
   The *Welshman* grows hot, and the *Irishman* huffs ;
The bonny bold *Scot* told the *Dutchman* he ly'd,
   A Word and a Blow, and so all went to Cuffs :
Coats were torn, and Heads were broken,
   Noses were Mawl'd, and Thumping went round ;
But in a while after, were forc'd to give quarter,
   And so went four Fools well beaten to Town.
     Coats were torn, &c.

An

An ODE,

Aluding to the Duke of MARLBOROUGH.

Set to Musick in two Parts.

ALBA Victorious, *Alba* fam'd in story,
    Still renown'd rightful Glory;
Alba Triumphant, Princes can Enthrone,
Hindred of their Lawful own:
So her Genius bright is soaring,
So confirm'd to her restoring.

Alba's Heroes conquer there,
Chiefly one beyond compare;
He that wonders he was Born,
To make blest, an Age forlorn:
Make his Native Land at home,
Ballance of all *Christendome.*

Thus as his sprightly Infancy was still inur'd to harms,
So was his Noble figure still adorn'd with double charms;
A gracious Aspect to subdue the Fair,
And Manly vigour to controul in War:
To crown the whole with blest Successes stor'd,
Divinely wise his Conduct still, and keen as Fate his
    Sword.

PUSS.

PUSS in a Corner.

A New SONG, *to a pretty New Tune made by a Man of Quality.*

TO Cullies and Bullies
    Of Country and Town,
To Wearers and Tearers
    Of Manteau and Gown ;
All Christian good People, that live round *Paul's*
    Steeple :
    I'll tell you a pleasant Case :
        Hot headed I wedded
        At Age of threescore,
    A flaunting young Wanton,
        Eighteen and no more ;
Of Parents I sought her, and Money soon bought her,
    I well might have had more Grace ;
        For daily at Table
        She'd pout and She'd squabble,
    And this still was all I got ;
        When e're I ask'd why,
        She'd cry pish, fie,
        For Gold nor Apparel
        I never did Quarrel,
    But only you starve my Cat.

A pretty young Kitty,
　　She had that could Purr ;
'Twas gamesome and handsome,
　　And had a rare Furr ;
And straight up I took it, and offer'd to stroake it,
　　In hopes I should make it kind :
　　But lowting and powting,
　　　　It still was to me,
　　Tho' Nature the Creature,
　　　　Design'd should be free,
I play'd with its Whiskers and would have had discourse,
　　But ah ! it was dumb and blind :
　When *Cloris* unquiet, who knew well its diet,
　　And found that I wanted that :
　　　Cry'd pray, Run, fetch *John*,
　　　He's the Man that can,
　　　When it does need it,
　　　Best knows how to feed it,
　Or gad you will starve my Cat.

　　As fleet as my Feet
　　　Could convey me I sped,
　　To *Johnny* who many
　　　Times Pussey had fed ;
I told him my Errand, he wanted no Warrant,
　　But hasted to shew his skill :
　　　He took it to stroak it,
　　　　And close in his Lap,
　　　He laid it to feed it,
　　　　And gave it some Pap,
And with such a passion it took the Collation,
　　Its Belly began to fill ;
And now within door is, so merry my *Cloris*,
　　She Laughs and grows wonderous Fat :
　　　And I run for *John*,
　　　Who's the Man that can,
　　　Tho' I'm at distance,
　　　Give present assistance,
　To please her, and feed her Cat.

The

The Loyal SCOT :

Or, the King's New Health, to a Scotch Tune.

Now

N OW the ground is hard Froze, and cawd Winter
    is come,
And our Master great *Willy* from *Holland's* got home ;
Now the Parliament Leards are set down to command,
Ise gang o're the *Tweed* into bonny *England* :
Ise oft heard of *Willy* in *Edinborough* Town,
Of his muckle great Deeds, and his gallant Renown ;
But I ne'er saw his Face yet, nor kiss'd his fair Hand,
So I'se gang for that Honour to bonny *England*.

To save us in season he cross'd o'er the Seas,
Turn'd out Popish Rats that were Eating our Cheese ;
Reliev'd us from *Rome* when we aw were trapann'd,
'Twas weel he came hither for bonny *England* :
He Fought for our Freedom, and finish'd the work,
He rooted out Mass, and he Licens'd the Kirk ;
He Peace too secur'd spight of all durst withstand,
For th' Profit and Honour of bonny *England*.

He Valourously, Valourously Life did expose,
Then generously, generously Guard him from Foes ;
Nea mear o'th' Army send heam, and disband,
Ye Deaughty Law makers of bonny *England* :
But merry, merry be, very merry ye Lads of *Whit-Hall*,
Sing derry, derry down, derry, derry down, derry,
    derry down all ;
And to Royal *Willy* take six in a Hand,
Ye Jolly brave Topers of bonny *England*.

A New SONG.

Made on the Nine and Twentieth of May, *at the raising the* Maypole *at ——— in honour of the Memory of K.* Charles *the Second's Restauration, and of the present Peace made by Her Sacred Majesty Queen* ANNE; *In three Movements.*

F*Lora*, beauteous Queen of *May*,
All the sprightly, fair and gay,
Summons this auspicious Day,
Here to act a Scene of Joy,
Ancient as the Siege of *Troy*,
So long renown'd in Story;
Grateful on a double score,
Since 'tis known in Times of *Yore*,
This blest Day did *Charles* restore,
And rais'd Triumphant *England's* Glory.

So in *Anna's* happy Reign
Glorious, far as flows the Main,
We a second Blessing gain;
Peace, our welcome Easer comes,
Round us verdant Olive blooms:
This Day once more renowning,
Peace should all with Joy inspire,
May it prove what we desire,
Praise shall charm each tuneful Lyre,
And Doubt for ever cease from frowning.

[*Second Movement;* swift.]

Then come merry boys,
Sing, dance, and rejoyce,
The *May-pole* let's raise
In honour of Peace,
And gratefully using the Blessings in store,
Remember the Rites of the Day heretofore.

As

As *Phillida* and *Johnny*
With Kisses sweet as Honey,
And others brisk and bonny,
Made loud their Joy at *Charles's* Restauration :
So let young *George* and *Jenny*,
And Lads and Lasses many,
To Peace, and Royal *Nanny*,
Devote the same, and crown the blest Occasion.

' The Pigg's MARCH.

A Song *for Mr.* Dogget, *in the Comical*
OPERA.

TRooping with bold Commanders,
   Dub, dub a dub, dub a dub, dub, dub,
   To charge our Foes,
   In Frost and Snows,
With hopes of Plunder big,
Late as we march'd thro' *Flanders*,
     Tantarra, rara, tantarra,
   Hunger and Cold
   Having made me bold,
In Knapsack I cramm'd a Pig a,
   Weeck, Weeck, Weeck, squeak'd the Pig,
   Ogh, Ogh, Ogh, grunts the Sow,
   And tho' swift away I fly,
   Yet she ran too as fast as I,
Scowring into an Alehouse,
   Dub, dub a dub, dub a dub, dub, dub,
   Where I for Shot
   Paid many a Pot,
And many had left on Score
Amongst my Comrades and Fellows ;
   Tantarra, rarra, tantarra,
        Scarce

Scarce with my Prize
Had I blest their Eyes,
But the Sow too was at the Door,
Weeck, Weeck, Weeck, squeaks the Pig,
Ogh, Ogh, Ogh, grunts the Sow,
Such Noises never heard before,
Set the House in a foul uproar.

Mawdlin the bouncing Hostess,
Dub, dub a dub, dub a dub, dub, dub,
Presently puffing came,
With a Face inflam'd,
And as red as a Rump of Beef,
Threatens me with a Justice,
Tantara, rara, tantarra,
'Till flat on the Ground,
I thump'd her down,
For daring to call me Thief,
Then Weeck, Weeck, loud she squeak'd,
Then *Ogh, Ogh,* like the Sow,
'Till at last in the woful fray,
My Pig too got quite away.

A New SONG.

Set to Musick by Mr. Thomas Farmer.

WHy ! why ! oh ye Pow'rs that rule the Sky !
   Must the lovesick *Damon* dye ?
When the Nymph is at ease, he admires ;
   She that causes my groaning,
   And kills with frowning,
For Love her hard Heart could never inspire :
Ah ! leave me to pain, still since 'tis in vain,
Still to perswade, or change the fair cruel Maid.
Like Men gazing on the Sun,
With too much Light am blind.

Soft as the tender moving Sighs,
  When longing Lovers meet ;
Like the divining Prophets wise,
  And like blown Roses sweet :
Modest, yet gay ; reserv'd, yet free ;
  Each happy Night a Bride ;
A Mein-like awful Majesty,
  And yet no spark of Pride.

The Patriarch, to gain a Wife,
  Chast beautiful, and young,
Serv'd fourteen Years a painful Life,
  And never thought 'em long.
Ah ! were you to reward such Cares,
  And Life so long could stay;
Not fourteen, but four hundred Years,
  Would seem but as one Day.

A

A Satyrical DITTY.

*Being the Poet's and Musician's Complaint
against the Lord Scrape, occasion'd by his
hindring the Performance of a Musical
ODE, made in Honour of King* GEORGE,
and set by Dr. Pepusch, *as well as other
tuneful Entertainments in the Hall on
the great* Coronation-Day.   *The Words
made to a pretty* Scotch *Tune, call'd,*
The Lass with the Golden Hair.

KIng *GEORGE* was crown'd with much Glory,
   And wonderful Joy did flow,
But yet I'll tell you a Story,
   Will scandalize all the Show :
The Peers, those Props of the Nation,
   In order all took their Post,
The Parties quite thro' the Nation,
   That Day neither gain'd, nor lost.

CHORUS.

But great Lord Scrape *was a Winner,
   Some threescore Pounds, or more,
For the King had no Musick at Dinner,
   The like never known before.*

Apollo strictly commanded,
   And Muses their Duty shew'd,
The Poet too had intended
   To publish a Royal *Ode;*
The Masters all had a meeting,
   With Voice, and *Treble,* and *Bass :*
But great Lord *Scrape* thought it fitting
   To let out for hire their place.

For

For he that hop'd to be Winner
  Of Threescore Pounds, or more,
Let the King have no Musick at Dinner,
  The like was ne'er known before.

Each Sheriff of the Town half fluster'd,
  Here's daily a tuneful Noise,
And the Mayor sits down to his Custard,
  With Musick to raise his Joys;
Nay, each dull Feast in the City
  The Fidlers will largely pay,
But the King had no Musick nor Ditty,
  On his Coronation Day;
For great Lord Scrape *would be winner*
  Of Threescore Pounds, and more,
So the King had no Consort at Dinner,
  The like was never before.

For which confounded Abuses,
  To all that write, play, or sing,
He'll still be scorn'd by the Muses,
  As well as the Court and King:
Love send his Wife more Caresses,
  Her Beauty was prais'd of late,
And nought but the Horn that she places
  Can suit his unmusical Pate;
Since great Lord Scrape *would be winner*
  Of Threescore Pounds and more,
And the King had no Musick at Dinner,
  Was ever the like before.

Whose chief Diversion neglected,
  We now the true Reason find,
What Musick can be expected
  From one of his *Tory* kind;
For he resolv'd to be Winner
  Of Threescore Pounds, and more,
So the King had no Musick at Dinner,
  Was ever the like before.

The

The KING's Health,

An ODE; *Perform'd before His Majesty King* William *at* Montague-house. *The Words made to an Excellent Tune of Mr.* Peasibles.

Loyal

Oyal *English* Boys, sing and Drink with pleasure,
  Bid your happy Land banish former fears ;
Revel in your Joys, give your Cups full measure,
  Cæsar's Fate commands all our future Years.

Jove and he govern the Affairs below here,
Earth and Sea own the force of their united power ;
Sound, sound Fame, through the spacious Universe his
    glory,
Cæsar's Name will for ever be the best in story.

Follow, follow, follow Sons of *Mars*,
  Bright Trophies of Honour reward ye ;
Follow, follow, follow to the Wars,
  Heav'n still will Guard ye,
Through the spacious Element of Air.

  Hark, hark ! how each Voice is extolling,
  How they Eccho from afar proud *France* is falling ;
  France, France is falling, *France, France* is falling,
Pride will soon, will soon, soon tumble down.

  Alass, how frail is Human pow'r ;
Founded on the moving Sands of vain Ambition,
  When perhaps the next sad hour
Tyrants feel the dreadful stroak of Revolution.

Ah ! how Happy then were *England's* jolly Swains,
That liv'd here at ease, when *Cæsar* took the Pains ?
Cæsar is the Star of our Renown,
  Cæsar is our safety and our Wealth ;
Fill then, fill up mighty Bowls all *Europe* round,
  And Kneel, and Drink his Health.

Pass about the Royal Bumper round,
  I O still to Godlike *Cæsar* sing ;
Whilst repeating Eccho's have no other sound,
  But long, long live the King,
  Long, long, long live the King.

A

A SONG.

Set to Musick by Dr. Crofts.

YE pretty Birds that Chirp and sing,
   Ye Trees and Plants that bud and grow,
Ye fragrant Flowers that bless the Spring,
   Tell me whence comes it you do so hark,
They answer, 'tis Cælestial Fire,
   The Gods call Love, the Gods call Love,
That does us all inspire.
   That Sacred Flame that sweetly charms
My Soul, when lovely *Cynthia* sings,
   That all Creations Labour warms,
And Nature to Perfection brings :

The buisy, useless Sun may cease to shine,
'Tis Love, 'tis Love, that sheds the Influence divine,
Then Lovers love on, and get Heaven betimes,
He that loves well atones for the worst of his Crimes ;
Jove locks up his Gate on the sordid and Base,
But the generous Lover is sure of a place ;
And the Nymph her Elizium need question no more,
When her Saint has a Key that can open the Door.

The Country Lass.

A New SONG.

DEar *Jemmy* when he sees me upon a Holiday,
　　When bonny Lads are easy, and all a dancing be
When Tiptoes are in fashion, and Loons will jump
　　and play,
Then he too takes Occasion to leer and ogle me,
He'll kiss my Hand with squeezing, whene'er he takes
　　my part,
　　　　But with each Kiss
　　　　He crowns my Bliss,
I feel him at my Heart.

But *Jockey* with his Cattle, and pamper'd Bags of Coyn,
Oft gave poor *Jemmy* Battle, whom feth I wish were
　　mine,
He tells me he is richer, and I shall ride his Mare,
That *Jemmy's* but a Ditcher, and can no Money spare ;
But welladay, my Fancy thinks more of *Jemmy's* Suit,
　　　　I take no Pride,
　　　　To Kirk to ride,
I'll gang with him a Foot.

Memorials of London *and* Westminster;
A Comical SATYR.   *The Words made to
a famous Tune, call'd,* Cook Laurel.

Come hither all you that love musical Sport,
  Ye Dons of the City, and Beaus of the Court,
I'll give ye a touch of my Lyrical Vein,
If you value plain Dealing shall entertain :

C H O R U S.

Oh London, *consider the blest Days of old,
When Labour brought Plenty, and Trading brought Gold,
When Ten Thousand Pounds was a King's Daughter's
      pay,
And Beef was a Feast on a Lord-Mayor's Day.*

I sing ye no News of what's won, or what's lost
Abroad, or what Wonders came over last Post,
Our Wars here are ended, and Peace now attones,
That Plague is blown off to the Northern Crowns ;
    *Then welfare the Court, and our Parliament-Men,
    Our Patrons at the Helm, who are now, or have been,
    Whilst th' Sword, Law, and Clergy, take Glasses in
        hand,
    A Health to our King, to our Church and Land.*

My

My Muse of the Gentry now chants out her Lay,
A Touch of the City Wits to by the way ;
She shews in a Comical Method unus'd,
How three Generations have both produc'd ;
  Oh London, *consider*, &c.

The Citizen he for his Son buys up Lands,
The Fop grows extravagant, drinks, whores and spends,
'Till dwindling at last the Estate is decay'd,
And his sneaking Heir forc'd to take a Trade ;
  Then welfare the Court, &c.

Tho' brisk City Dames too the Courtier oft gets,
The Wittals still wriggate into their Estates,
Whose Offspring degrade from the Gentleman's Stem,
Whilst tothers turn Courtiers, and cuckold them ;
  Oh London, *consider*, &c.

Since Difference so little then lyes on Record,
'Twixt those of the Apron, and those of the Sword,
Let's canvass their Humours, from great to the small,
We sprung from Old *Adam*, the Gardener all ;
  Then welfare the Court, &c.

Great Noblemen, Commoners, Lawyers, and Priests,
You daily may find in the Court of Requests,
All buzzing about in that great Hive of Bees,
With different Intentions to lade their Thighs ;
  But welfare the Court, &c.

What News is the quæry, what Factions oppose,
What Places are vacant, and when the King goes ;
How far he has Power in the Grants of his Land,
And if they may take without Reprimand ;
  Then welfare the Court, &c.

But now, as 'tis reason, let's cry up each House,
For Justice late done a great Peer and his Spouse,
The D—— from the Bar a brisk Batchelor's gone,
And she's a pure Virgin for all Sir *John ;*
  Then welfare the Court, &c.

H 2

The

The City's disturb'd too, and Anger does rowse,
About an Elopement of one from her Spouse,
What Wives are cry'd down, and what happens thereon,
You'll certainly hear in the next Post-Man;
   Then welfare the Court, &c.

And now we're in *London* let's pass this Affair,
And praise the good Prætor now sits in the Chair;
Tho' stubborn Opinions late pester'd the Hall,
Our Orthodox Party now graces St. *Paul's;*
   Oh London, *consider*, &c.

Not so was *Sir *Numps*, whom I owe an old Score,
For basely affronting me once at his Door;
The Poet was routed because of his Pen,
For fear he should lampoon his Tribe within;
   Oh London, *consider*, &c.

The Chandlers he mawl'd, and the Bakers he stript,
Damn'd Rogues he conniv'd at, the Beggars he whipt,
The Meeting fill'd, and by Law made it out,
But the honest old Custard Cap fac'd about;
   Oh London, *consider*, &c.

But now we all hope we shall see a glad Day,
When *Church* and *Dissenters* in Union obey;
The City's well Ruler his Time well employs,
In a Work that would make all the Land rejoyce;
   Oh London, *consider*, &c.

Our Sheriff had late in his Scutheon a Blot,
By some who imagin'd his Purse was too fat;
The Scale was just turn'd up by one honest Peer,
The Poor else had lost a good Friend this Year;
   Then welfare the Court, &c.

---

* *Sir* H. E.

His

His Colleague too, who is oft given to treat
His Country Men *Britains* with Wine and good Meat,
Had late an odd Compliment, scarce for his Ease,
For touching the Province of Leeks and Cheese ;
　　But welfare the Court, &c.

The next let us give the Exchange a dry Bob,
Where Fools manage Bargains by way of Stock-jobb,
When all their whole Profit at last they will find,
They may put in their Eyes, and yet ne'er be blind ;
　　Oh London, *consider,* &c.

The Companies, who so much Bustle have made,
Which has the best Right in *East-India* to trade,
The one, a Success that they ever might boast,
The baiting the Tyger most wisely lost ;
　　Oh London, *consider,* &c.

The tother who jocundly laugh'd at that sport,
Were lately too baulk'd of their Fancy at Court ;
The King who for Union had set down his Rules,
In short bid 'em quarrel no more like Fools ;
　　Then welfare the Court, &c.

And thus I think proper to finish my Shew,
For now methinks *Pegasus* gallops but slow ;
Be loyal and wise, and like Friends all agree,
Your Airs are *safe by your Fleet at Sea ;
　　Then welfare the Court and our Parliament-Men,
　　Our Patrons at Helm, who are now, or have been ;
　　Let the Sword, Law, and Clergy take Glasses in hand,
　　A Health to our King, our Church and Land.

---

* *Bishop of* Salisb.

The

The New *Windsor* BALLAD.

*The Muse complaining and making Satyri-
cal Remarks upon Sir* Jan Brazen, *a
Man in Office there.   The Words made
in Imitation of the Old famous Ballad of
King* Arthur *and his Knights,* viz. St.
George *he was for* England, &c.

To tell a Tale of *Windsor* my Muse is now inclin'd,
   Where who will choose his Company may
      Whigg and *Tory* find,
But that I pass at present by to treat of other News,
How Sir *Jan*, Sir *Jan*, no dinner gave a Muse.

CHORUS.

The rest treat all Men civilly, Sir Jan *has no such
      Sence,*
Sing *honi Soit qui mal y pense.*

The Queen, th' Almighty bless Her, the Purse does
      open wide,
And with good store of Dishes for the Greencloth
      does provide,
To treat all Strangers heartily, *Turk, Christian*, or the
      Jews;
But Sir *Jan*, Sir *Jan*, &c.
      The rest treat all Men civilly, &c.

The Gentlemen the Waiters gave all a chearful Look,
And *Lowman* kindly ordered well the Butler and the
      Cook,
Nor 'mongst their Favour did I want my good Old
      Friend *Randues;*
      The rest treat all Men civilly, &c.

Perhaps tho' in another Case this may be taken right,
That he would shew no Countenance, least he a Bard
      should fright;
It must be so, no other way he can himself excuse;
Since Sir *Jan*, Sir *Jan*, &c.
      The rest treat all Men civilly, &c.

A Muse a sort of Creature is that likes not every head,
A therefore as some Courtiers think not worthy to be
      fed,
A Head I mean, with Face that wears red Pimples,
      green and blews,
Like Sir *Jan*, Sir *Jan*, &c.
      The rest treat all Men civilly, &c.

To

To mend this damn'd Complection then I'd have him
    get it sowct,
For if the Flame increases still 'twill shortly burn each
    Toast,
And then each Pen that dips in Ink will scrawl in
    sharp Abuse,
On Sir *Jan*, Sir *Jan*, &c.
    The rest treat all Men civilly, &c.

This Knight but little is we find oblig'd to Nature's
    Care,
In Youth a nauseous flashy Fop, in elder Days a Bear,
Who if he is not burnishing thinks he all's Time does
    lose,
For Sir *Jan*, Sir *Jan*, &c.
    The rest treat all Men civilly, &c.

He freely told his Friends at Court no Place for him
    was fit,
But where he still might cram his Mace, and have no
    use of Wit,
And now he sits from Morn to Night, and gorges till
    he spews,
Where Sir *Jan*, Sir *Jan*, &c.
    The rest treat all Men civilly, &c.

Instead of Conversation good that should be there
    serene,
He eats and drinks, and puffs and stinks in honour of
    the Queen ;
And if he's ever civil, 'tis to those with ruby Heroes
But Sir *Jan*, Sir *Jan*, &c.
    The rest treat all Men civilly, &c.

So Knight farewel, and prithee hast down to Old
    Nick thy Uncle,
Where thou a Title new shalt have, *The Knight of the
    Carbuncle;*
                                'Tis

"Tis thine as soon as of thy coming there they hear
    the News,
Because *Jan*, Sir *Jan*, no Dinner gave a Muse ;
    The rest treat all Men civilly, Sir Jan *he has no Sense,*
Sing *Honi soit qui mal y pense.*

A SONG *in a New* Opera : *The Words
alluding to the happy Conjugal Love between Her Majesty, and the P——— of*
Denmark.

M*Irtillo* Darling of kind Fate,
    Dear *Mirtillo,* good as great ;
And what's wond'rous as 'tis true,
Darling of my People too :
Ever, ever has been known,
Kind to me, and Me alone.

Many pledges of our Love,
Giv'n and since receiv'd by *Jove ;*
Made our Constant passion strong,
Firm and perfect as 'twas long :
But what most my Joy did crown,
He was Mine, and Mine alone.

Tho' grand Cares disturb'd my peace,
Still *Mirtillo* gave me ease ;
Were he Sick, I lost all Joy,
Were he Well, still so was I :
And what's dearer than My Throne,
Mine He was, and Mine alone.

Glo-

Gloriana's *Resentment, for her Lord's going so often to the Wars.*

A SONG.

Igh Renown and Martial Glory,
  Fate all owes this happy Year,
To fill the Leaves of *Britain's* Story,
  Victoria lays before ye Oaken Boughs,
Form'd into Wreathes to crown great *Strephon's* Brows ;
  Yet though Wars alarming
Please the Sons of Fame,
  Conquest too be charming,
Sounding *Strephon's* Name ;
      Fear blasts my Joys,
      And fills with Tears my Eyes,
      To know and grieve me,
      He so soon must leave me.

A

A Welcome to the Happy Peace,

A New SONG.

NOW comes joyful Peace,
    And happy Days the Times will turn,
Nor shall we mourn
In Doubt forlorn,
  But live at Ease.
Drums and Trumpets sounds,
With War and Wounds,
That us'd to rore,
And soil with Gore,
The *Flemish* Shore,
  All now must cease ;
Fate does smile at last,
Whilst we find Joy
Attoning for the Troubles past.

When the *German* Head,
His Eagle spread,
With *Spanish* Loggs,
And *Hogan* Hoggs,
With all their Froggs
  Seem to oppose :
We who still advise
With some as wise,
If Queens can tell,
What Heads excell,
And counsel well,
  Must think 'em Foes.
Fears will end at last,
Whilst we find Joy
Attoning for the Troubles past.

The

The Female Quarrel :

Or a Lampoon upon Phillida *and* Chloris.
*The Words made to the Tune of a Coun-
try Dance, call'd,* A Health to *Betty.*

O F all our modern Storys
   To Minuets sung, or Borees,
    None stir the Mood,
    As late the Feud,
'Twixt *Phillida* and *Chloris.*

Two Lasses brisk and young, Sir,
And dear Companions long, Sir,
    As News now goes,
    Turn mortal Foes,
About a bawdy Song, Sir.

'Twas *Phillida* the Airy,
Well fac'd, but wondrous hairy,
    This Sonnet sent,
    With kind Intent,
To make her Neighbour merry.

But

But *Chloris* on th' Occasion,
Believing Reputation
      Was stabb'd and gor'd,
      And prick'd and bor'd,
Thus broke out into Passion.

Chloris.
I know thou hast been watching,
And this Affront been hatching,
      Long time with Shame
      To blast my Fame,
And hinder me from matching.

Your proud, ill Nature,
Which slights each Creature,
      Yet all suppose,
      In Corner close,
No Doxy likes Man better.

And tho' you seem'd to drive all,
And of Embrace deprive all,
      Old thirty five
      Had got a Wife,
But for the Lap-dog Rival.

Affection had been dawning,
And he e'er this been spawning,
      Like Am'rous Frog,
      Had not Sir Dog
With licking charm'd, and fawning.

But Fortune was his Debtor,
And since has sped him better,
      Whilst frekish Shrew,
      And foolish Beau,
Put on the Wedlock Fetter.

And tho' you think there's scarce one
For me to wipe mine A—— on,
      To purge my Sins,
      And buy me Pins,
I've nigled an Old Parson.

My

My Coach he does provide too,
In which at Ease we ride too,
    Whilst you can't eat,
    You lace so strait,
To shew a Shape as I do.

This Lash that deep did come Sir,
Poor *Philly* cut so home Sir,
    She swell'd her Lungs,
    And vow'd her Wrongs
Not longer should be dumb Sir,

Ye Jilt, she cry'd, what Pother
You make your Tricks to smother,
    If any Wrong
    Be in the Song,
Go home and ask your Mother.

It might, though you are sullen,
Be sung by *Anna Bullen*,
    Ask Father *Wise*,
    That Bedrid lyes,
Or else dear Draper Woolen.

Whose Yard, when she's at leasure,
Is us'd her Cloth to measure,
    And often try'd,
    Sometimes for Pride,
And sometimes for her Pleasure.

Enquire of Husband *Testy*,
Or Son-in-Law that kiss'd ye,
    Who boldly swears
    He'll get him Heirs,
Whene'er his Dad grows resty.

For Learning well may lack too
A Cullise for the Back too,
    And ne'er prevail,
    To cure thy Ail,
Tho' he's both Priest and Quack too.

But

But Fame no more is reaching,
Then you will dance with teaching,
    As much you'll get
    With your splay Feet,
As he with bungling Preaching.

His Precept, or his Potion,
Is sure to give a Motion,
    Yet all his Skill
    You'll find is still,
A meer, and empty Notion.

And thus concludes the Tattle,
Which o'er the Town did rattle,
    Two Days, perhaps,
    If they relapse,
May bring it to a Battle.

Mr. DOGGETT's 2d Song *in the*
Comick Opera.

M*Undunga* was as feat a Jade,
  As e'er was in our Town;
And I a Jolly lusty Lad,
  As e'er mow'd Clover down:
So close three Years we ty'd the Knot,
Our thumping Hearts went pit, pit pat,
And mine so pleas'd with you know what,
  We thought of nothing else:
Sing whim wham, whim wham, whim wham sing,
Whilst ding dong, ding dong, ding dong ding,
  Ding, ding dong rung the Bells.

Her Nose was long, and stood awry,
  A goodly fruitful sign;
Nor blam'd I rotten Teeth close by,
  Because the case was mine:
Her feet were Splay, my Leggs were Warpt,
We were so match'd we never Carpt,

I 2

Whilst

Whilst merrily Blind *Tom* that Harp'd,
  In Tune our story tells :
Sing whim wham, whim wham, whim wham sing,
Whilst ding dong, ding dong, ding dong ding,
  Ding, ding dong rung the Bells.

Brave times were these, but ah ! how soon,
  Do Wedlock Comforts fall ;
The days that then were hony Moon,
  Are Wormwood now and Gall :
Her Tongue clacks louder then a Mill,
No longer do we Buss or Bill,
But Jangle like two Fiends of Hell,
  Broke out from flaming Cells :
And whim wham, whim wham, whim wham sing,
Nor ding dong, ding dong, ding dong ding,
  No longer ring the Bells.

The Second SONG *in the Second* Act ; *Sung by one Representing* Hymen. *Set by Mr*. Courtivil.

HERE is *Hymen*, here am I,
  Some Mens Grief, and some Mens Joy;
Here's for Better and for Worse,
Many Bless, and many Curse.

Tender Virgins soft and young,
You that to be Mothers long;
By my aid Love's raptures try,
Save your Blushes, save your blushes,
Save your Blushes and enjoy.

A New DIALOGUE : *Set to the Tune of* Cavililly Man. *Between* Tom *stitch the Taylor, and* Kate *Stroaker Dairy-maid : To be Sung by Mr.* Pinkethman, *and* Mrs. Willis, *He carrying a pair of Shears, and she her Knitting work.*

Tom.   **B**Right Honour provokes me, farewel jolly Kate,
For to morrow I must to the Wars begone ;
Such noble Cunnundrums do buz in my Pate,
I must lay by my Shears, and turn Gentleman.

Kate. You promis'd me Marriage, you scoundrel ye did,
And swore by your Goose, it should soon be done ;
Tom. What, do as the Taylors do, Heaven forbid,
I must now break my Oath, like a Gentleman.

Kate. Well, nothing comes on't, and I care not a Louse,
For I'll soon be a very good Maid again ;
With *Ralph, Kit,* and *Harry,* sing dance & carouse,
The whilst you turn a wooden legg'd Gentleman.

Tom.

Tom. I'll meet with three Boys too that make the
       World ring,
Bold *Marlborough*, brave *Stanhope*, and great *Eugene;*
I'll go to their Tents, and I'll dine like a King,
  And then who knows *Tom* stitch from a Gentleman.

Kate. Good lack, who's that *Marlbrough* that makes
       such a rout,
  And what's that same *Hugeone*, the Volk so praise ;
Tom. Two that chop up more kickshaws at one Fighting
       bout,
  Then a Taylor at dinner can Beans or Peas ;

Kate. The Fame of this *Marlbrough* all *Kersendom* fills,
  And that *Hugeone* too, ever renown'd will be ;
Tom. That can Climb over Mountains, o'er Rocks and
       high Hills,
  Just as quick as a Cat up a Wallnut Tree.

Kate. He can leap up to Honour as high as the Moon,
Tom. Ay, and down through the Deeps of the Sea
       below ;
Like a Dragon spit fire on the Ships at *Thoulon*,
  And confound all the *French* at one fatal blow.

Kate. The *Mounsieur* still brags that he'll lead 'em a
       dance,
  But that's the *French* Maggot well known before ;
Tom. Whilst we with our Troops are invading of *France*,
  Th' old Fool with *Te Deums* makes *Paris* roar.

Kate. Adzooks 't has half made me wish I were a Man,
  To be bouncing and handling of Balls of Lead ;
Tom. Dar'st thou prate of venturing to let off a Gun,
  Why a Pistol thus long, Fool, would fright thee dead.

Kate. You talk like a Novice, faith *Tomas* you do,
  A yard Musquet would scarce be an Inch too long ;
To prove't I'll get Arms, and go ramble with you,
  And then down with the *French* shall be all our Song.
                             Tom.

Tom. If this thou canst do Girl, I'll prime thy Fire-lock.
Kate. And I'll empty your Bandaleers soon again ;
Tom. I'll put thee on Breeches, and tuck up thy Smock,
    And we'll March both together like Gentlemen.

Tom. O'er Mountain o'er Valley, *French* bougers to fight,
Kate. All day with our Snapsacks we'll trudge along ;
        We'll seek out a Barn,
Tom. And we'il pig there at night,
    And still down with the *French* shall be all our Song.

Tom. Let's Dance then for Joy of merry new match,
Kate. What could we do else that are brisk and young ;
Tom. And tho' with our Mirth we a little One hatch,
Kate. Yet still down with the *French* shall be all our
        song.

CHORUS of both.

And tho' with our Mirth we a little One hatch,
Yet still down with the French *shall be all our Song.*

A SONG, *being a Musical Lecture to my
Countrymen. Sung in my last benefit
Play by Mr.* Birkhead ; *the Tune within
the Compass of the Flute.*

YE *Britains*, how long shall I tire my Brains
With Politick study, the worst of all Pains?
      To teach ye Uniting,
      From Jarring and Fighting,
And crown all your days with Peace:
I've shewn in some Rhimes that have made ye laugh,
More truth then some Black-coats have Preach'd by
      half;
      Who still are assisting,
      To vouch non-resisting,
From whence all our feuds increase.

But

But if ye all raving Confusion made,
  And nothing but Discord saw;
        Y'are roaring and yelling,
        And daily Rebelling,
  Without any Reason or Law:
For all that the rule of our Monarch evade,
  Who is Protestant honest and true;
Will Moaning, and Groaning, see Asses, sing Masses,
  When ever they bring in a New.

Yet lately we saw the rough *H—land* Bears,
All clattering their Targets about our Ears;
        All Union rejecting,
        So long in effecting,
    Inflam'd with a Frantic Zeal:
They want a new King, that will mend their fare,
That Butter no longer may choak with Hair;
        Their Oatmeal and Water,
        And what follows after,
  Coarse Bannocks of Barly meal.

But for all they were baffled, our hopeful Land,
  That ever will Faction breed;
        To keep up the story,
        Of High-flying *Tory*,
  Have brought on the Crazy brain'd *S—d:*
Whose Ministry whom the Pretenders maintain'd,
  By thousands from such as Rebel;
        To mend the disaster,
        Of bringing their Master,
  Wou'd bring in the Devil of Hell.

The Consolatory Muse, *to a great Lady at* Court, *a* SONNET : *Occasion'd by the scurrilous affrontive Papers, lately cry'd up and down the Streets. The Words fitted exactly to the* Italian *Air of fair* Dorinda, *in the* Opera *of* Camilla.

SMile *Lucinda*, Revel with thy happy Race,
  Great *Clorona*, ne'er will fail to do thee grace ;
    Wisely slight,
    The vulgar's spight,
For the Trifle of their hate,
All must suffer, who are destin'd to be great.

    Just and Loyal,
Render duty more and more ;
    Great as Royal,
She has new rewards in store :
    Tho' the Crowd
    Do rail aloud,
Nought thy pleasure shall untune ;
Smile *Lucinda*, envious Currs will bay the Moon.

    Thus with Glory,
Sounded by the Trump of Fame ;
    Shall your story,
Flourish with your Hero's name :
    You and he,
    By Fates decree,
And Divine *Clorona's* grace ;
Shall the Favourites of all former times surpass.

The Duke of ORMOND'S *Health : Set by*
Mr. J. Barrett.

N *Eptune* frown, and *Boreas* roar,
   Let thy Thunder bellow ;
Noble *ORMOND's* now come o'er,
   With each gallant *English* fellow :
      Then to welcome him a shore,
      To his Health a brimmer pour,
Till every one be mellow,
Remembring *Rodondello,* remembring *Rodondello,*
Remembring, remembring *Rodondello,*
Remembring, remembring *Rodondello.*

Tho' at *Cales* they scap'd our Guns,
   By strong wall'd umbrello;
Civil Jarrs and Plundring Dons,
   Curse upon the metal yellow :
      Had the valiant Duke more Men,
      He a Victor there had been,
As late at *Rodondello,*
As late, &c.

Mounsieur and Petite *Anjou,*
   Plot your state Intrigo :
Take new Marshall *Chateaurenault,*
   Then consult with *Spanish Deigo :*
      And new Glory to advance,
      Sing *Te Deum* through all France,
Pour la Victoire at *Vigo,*
Pour la, *&c.*

We

We mean while to crown our Joy,
  Laughing at such folly,
To their Health full Bowls employ,
  Who have cur'd our Melancholy :
    And done more to furnish Tales,
    Now at *Vigo*, then at *Cales*,
Fam'd *Essex* did, or *Rawleigh*,
Brave Essex, &c.

Great *Eliza* on the Main,
  Quell'd the Dons Boastado ;
In Queen *ANN's* Auspicious Reign,
  Valour conquers, not Bravado :
    Come but such another Year,
    We the spacious Sea shall clear,
Of *French* and *Spains* Armado,
Of French, &c.

Once more then tho' *Boreas* roar,
  And loud Thunder bellow ;
Since Great *ORMOND* is come o'er,
  With each gallant *English* fellow :
    Let us welcome all a Shore,
    To each Health a brimmer pour,
Till every one be mellow,
Remembring *Rodondello*, &c.

A DIALOGUE *between a* French *Beau, and a*
Coquett de Angletere.

Beau. WHEN vile *Stella* kind and *tendre*,
      Recompense *five le Amour ;*
    You mine Heart have made me *rendre*,
      If yours come not in *Retour :*
    Black despair I can't *defendre*,
    No, no, no I can't *defendre*,
    Grief must kill me *tout les Jours.*

                              Coq.

Coq. How can *Damon* Love another,
　　Who believes himself so fine ;
　He may talk and keep a pother,
　　But to change can ne'er incline :
　So much Charm must slight all other,
　Ay, ay, ay must slight all other,
　　He believes himself so fine.

Beau. Then adieu false *Esperanza,*
　　Tout les Plaisirs de Beau *Jours ;*
　Stella's Heart keeps at distance,
　　And disdains *le Cher* effort :
　She *mon Ame* will ne'er advance,
　No, no, no will ne'er advance,
　　Cruel Death then *prend mon Ceur.*

Coq. You a *Beau,* and talk of dying,
　　'Tis a Cheat I'll ne'er believe ;
　You've such Life in Self enjoying,
　　Death's a word you can't forgive :
　Go improve Deceit and Lying,
　Ay, ay, ay but name no dying,
　　That's a Cheat I'll ne'er believe.

CHORUS.

He. When, when will you prove me, to know
　The truth of a Passionate *Beau ;*
She. How, how shall I prove ye, to know
　The truth of a flashy Town *Beau ;*
He. By the Sighs, and the Tears, of the wretch,
She. By his Paint, and his Powder and Patch ;
He. By his Mouth, and his very good Teeth,
She. By his Nose, and his very bad Breath ;
He. By his Eyes, and the Air of his Face,
She. When he Oagles, and looks like an Ass ;
He. Par Dieu ma Avere, each part my truth will shew,
She. Morbleau mon fou, I never can think so.

Pretty

Pretty PEGG *of* Wandsor.

THE Infant Spring was shining,
　　With Greens and Cowslips gay,
The Sun was just declining,
To Bath him in the Sea :

When

When as o'er *Wandsor* Hill I pass'd,
  To view the prospect rare,
A lovely Lass sat on the Grass,
  Whose Breath perfum'd the Air.
No more let Fame advance, Sir,
  In *London Jenny's* praise ;
For pretty *Pegg* of *Wandsor*,
  Excells her a Thousand ways :
      For Face, for Skin,
      For Shape, for Mein,
For Charming, charming Smile ;
      For Eye, and Thigh,
      And something by,
A King would give an Isle.
The Courtier for her favour,
  Would slight his Golden claims ;
The *Jacobite* to have her,
  Would quite Abjure King *JAMES ;*
      The ruddy plump Judge,
      That Circuit's do's trudge,
Would managing Tryals defer ;
      Post-pone a Cause,
      And wrest the Laws,
To get but the managing her.
The General would leave Bombing,
  Of Towns in hot Campaigns ;
The Bishop his vum and Thumbing,
  And plaguing his Learned Brains :
      One fighting would mock,
      And tother his Flock,
A pin for Religion or *France ;*
      This shun the Wars,
      And that his Prayers,
If *Peggy* but gave a Glance.
The powder'd Playhouse Ninny,
  With much less Brains than Hair,
That deals with *Moll* and *Jenny,*
  And tawdry common Ware :

If *Peggy* once he,
Saw under a Tree,
With rosie Chaplets crown'd ;
He'd roar, and scow'r,
And Curse the hour,
That e'er he saw *London* Town.

The Sailor us'd to Slaughter,
In Ships of Oak strong wall'd ;
Whose Shot 'twixt Wind and Water,
The *French jam foutres* mawl'd :
If *Peggy* once there,
Her Vessel should steer,
And give the rough Captain a blow ;
He'd give his Eyes,
And next *French* Prize,
That he might but thump her so.

The Doctor her half Sainted,
For Cures controuling Fate ;
That has warm Engines planted,
At many a Postern gate :
If *Peggy* once were ill,
And wanted his Skill,
He'd soon bring her to Death's door :
By Love made blind,
Slip from behind,
And make his Injection before.

The Cit that in old *Sodom*,
Sits Cheating round the Year ;
And to my Lord, and Madam,
Puts off his Tarnisht ware :
This sneaking young Fop,
Would give his whole Shop,
To get pretty *Peggy's* good will ;
To have her stock,
So close kept Lock'd,
And put in a Key to her Till.

Yet

Yet tho' she Hearts disposes,
    And all things at her point ;
Tho' *London Jenny's* Nose is,
    Like others out of Joynt :
        Yet she has one fault,
        Which *Jenny* has not,
Who Loves happy Laws has obey'd ;
    For *Peggy* does slight,
    And starve her delight,
To keep the dull Name of a Maid.

A Song : *To a young* Lady, *Affronted by an Envious old Woman.*

IN vain, in vain fantastick Age,
    Thou seek'st such Virtue to abuse ;
Ophelia does Mankind engage,
    Each valiant Sword, each noble Muse :
Frantick with spite, let crazy Time,
    Take pleasure to ingender strife ;
Whilst blooming Beauty in her Prime,
    Takes with a Gust the Joys of Life.

Each shameful word that Malice speaks,
    Adds, dearest Charmer, to your Fame ;
Each hallow'd Grove loud Eccho makes,
    Resounding fair *Ophelia's* Name :
Old age does Beauty still prophane,
    Age ever did good Nature want ;
By Scandal you more Glory again,
    'Tis Persecution makes the Saint.

Lon-

LONDON'S Loyalty.

ROuse up great Genius of this potent Land,
  Lest Traytors once more get the upper hand ;
The Rebel crowd their former Tenets own,
And Treasons worse than Plagues infect the Town :
The sneaking *May'r*, and his two pimping *Sheriffs*,
Who for their Honesty no better are then Thieves ;
Fall from their Sov'raign's side to court the *Mobile*,
Oh ! *London, London*, where's thy Loyalty ?

First, *Yorkshire Patience* twirls his Copper Chain,
And hopes to see a *Commonwealth* again ;
The sneaking Fool of breaking is afraid,
Dares not change sides for fear he loose his Trade :
Then Loyal *Slingsby* does their *Fate Divine* ——
He that Abjur'd the *King*, and all his Sacred Line ;
And is suppos'd his Father's Murd'rer to be,
Oh ! *Bethel, Bethel*, where's thy Loyalty ?

A most notorious Villain late was caught,
And after to the Bar of Justice brought ;
But *Slingsby* pack'd a Jury of his own,
Of worser Rogues then e'er made Gallows groan :
Then *Dugdale's* Evidence was soon decry'd,
That was so just and honest, when old *Stafford* dy'd ;
Now was a Rogue, a perjur'd Villian and he ly'd,
Oh ! Justice, Justice, where's thy Equity ?

Next *Cl—ton* murmurs Treason unprovok'd,
He supp'd the King, and after wish'd him choak'd ;
'Cause *Danby's* Place was well bestow'd before,
He Rebel turns, seduc'd by Scarlet Whore :
His sawcy Pride aspires to high Renown,
Leather Breches are forgot in which he trudg'd to
      Town ;
Nought can please the scribling Clown but th'
      Treasury,
Oh ! *Robert, Robert*, where's thy Modesty ?

                              Pl——er

Pl —— er now grows dull, and pines for want of
    Whore,
Poor *Creswel,* she can take his word no more ;
Three hundred Pounds is such a heavy Yoke,
Which not being paid, the worn-out Baud is broke :
These are the Instruments by Heaven sent,
These are the Saints Petition for a *Parliament ;*
That would for Int'rest-sake destroy the Monarchy,
Oh ! *London, London,* where's thy Loyalty ?

Heaven bless fair *England,* and its Monarch here,
And *Scotland* bless your High Commissioner ;
Let *Perkin* his ungracious Error see,
And *Tony* 'scape no more the Triple-Tree :
Then Peace and Plenty shall our Joys restore,
Villains and Factions shall oppress the Town no more ;
But every Loyal Subject then shall happy be,
Nor need we care for *London's* Loyalty.

The Law of Nature; A SONG *Set to an Excellent new Tune.*

WHilst their Flocks were feeding,
        Near the foot of a flowry Hill ;
Celladon complaining of his Fate,
        Thus to *Astrea* cry'd ;
Hear my gentle pleading,
    Ah ! cruel Nymph forbear to kill
A Shepherd with disdain and hate,
        Whom you have once enjoy'd ;
There is a Sacred pow'r in Love,
Is beyond all Moral rules :
    Follow the Laws of Nature,
    For the Divine Creator
            Did produce,
            And for Human use,
            Did Beauty choose,
Who deny themselves are Fools :

                                Every

Every Heart is pair'd above,
  And Ingratitude's a Sin :
      To all the Saints so hateful,
      She that is found ingrateful,
      May too late,
      In a wretched State,
      Knock at Heaven's Gate,
  But shall never enter in.

Had our first made Father,
  Lord of the whole Creation,
Done such a Crime as could have damn'd us all,
      In trespassing on his Wife :
  Heaven, no doubt, had rather,
      When it the ill design had known,
Have plac'd his Angel ere the Fall,
      Guarding the Tree of Life ;
But he that well knew *Adam's* Breast,
  Whom Nature learnt to wooe,
          Never intended Damming,
          Nor did the Serpents shamming,
              Edifie ;
      For the Bone of his side,
      That was made his Bride,
  Taught him what he was to do :
Nor was the Maker e'er possess'd,
  With Rage that he did enjoy ;
  But the Reflection hated,
  What he with pains Created,
      Should be thought,
      Such a cowardly Sot,
      To be poorly caught,
  In such a sneaking Lye.

The Curtain LECTURE.

A New SONG.

He. OF all Comforts I miscarried,
      When I play'd the Sot and married;
  'Tis a Trap there's none need doubt on't,
  Those that are in't will fain get out on't:
She. Fye, my Dear, pray come to bed,
  That Napkin take and bind your Head,
  Too much drink your Brain has dos'd,
  You'll be quite alter'd when repos'd.

He. Oons, tis all one, if I'm up or lye down,
  For as soon as the Cock crows I'll be gone,
She. 'Tis to grieve me, thus you leave me,
  Was I, was I made a Wife to lye alone.

He. From your Arms my self divorcing,
  I this Morn must ride a Coursing,
  Sport that far excels a Madam,
  Or all Wives have been since *Adam.*

She. I

She. I, when thus I've lost my due,
    Must hug my Pillow wanting you,
    And whilst you tope all the Day,
    Regale in Cups of harmless Tea.

He. Pox what care I, drink your Slops 'till you dye,
    Yonder's Brandy will keep me a Month from home,
She. If thus parted, I'm broken hearted,
    When I, when I send for you, my dear pray come.

He. E're I'll be from rambling hindred,
    I'll renounce my Spouse and Kindred,
    To be sober I have no leasure,
    What's a Man without his Pleasure.
She. To my Grief then I must see,
    Strong Ale and Nantz my Rivals be,
    Whilst you tope it with your Blades,
    Poor I sit stitching with my Maids.

He. Oons you may go to your Gossips you know,
    And there if you can meet a Friend, pray do ;
She. Go you Joker, go Provoker,
    Never, never shall I meet a Man like you.

A

A Royal SONG.

On the King of Great Britian's *going: In two Movements. The Words Set to a Tune of my own.*

STeer, steer the Yacht to reach the strand,
    Since *Cæsar* will be gone ;
And proclaims our cloudy Land,
    So long to lose the Sun.

Now, now Great *Wallia* brightly shine,
    And with sole order sway ;
To shew with Royalty divine,
    What comes another day.

Whilst Royal *GEORGE* on foaming Seas,
To give his harrass'd Empire ease,
        Consulting Foreign Kings,
        Will do us Glorious things,
Which timely shall appear,
As well abroad as here,
When *Hanover* regales this happy Year.

[*Second Movement.*]

Whilst the gay Summer cloys us with Roses,
    Woodbine and Jessamine feast the Sence ;
Whilst the Rebellion's gone, each supposes,
    Tho' some *Scotch* Loons they say make pretence :
Mackintosh, Mackintosh, Rebel and Looby,
Bring again home again, *Foster* the Booby ;
        Think there's a Season,
        Once to do reason,
Then for your sakes, we'll clear the rest.

The Authentick Letter of Marshal de Boufflers, *to the* French *King, on the late
unfortunate, but glorious Battle (as he
calls it) near* Mons, *paraphrastically done
into Metre in broken* English.   *Set to a
famous Tune on the* Welch *Harp.*

Harp.

Harp.

M E send you, Sir, one Letter,
  Me vish it were a better,
    And here me write
    Of our last Fight,
And who vas Conquest getter.

Dame

Dame Fortune was a Jilt, Sir,
Dat so much Blood is spilt, Sir,
    We own our Loss,
    But yet it was
A noble, glorious Tilt, Sir.

And do de Field by deyrs, Sir,
As now it plain appears, Sir,
    So brave and stout,
    De *French* ne'er fought,
Morbleu dis Hunder Years, Sir.

Villars and I long stood, Sir,
Encamp'd within a Wood, Sir,
    He Left, I Right,
    Where we did fight,
As long as e'er we could, Sir.

And to affright, like Giants,
And offer dire Defiance,
    Fearless to dye,
    In Works Nose high,
We ventur'd bold as Lyons.

But d' Enemy broke troo, Sir,
As dey are us'd to do, Sir,
    And made us flinch
    From treble Trench,
Begar, me tell you true, Sir.

And manfully retiring,
To scape de plaguee Firing,
    We wheel'd about,
    And sav'd a Rout,
To all de Warlds admiring.

Villars i'th' Knee vas wounded,
By Horse and Foot surrounded,
    And of my Hurt
    You'll have Report,
As soon as me have found it.

In

In Heel, dey say's my Blow, Sir,
Achilles vas hurt so, Sir,
    De Deevil and all
    Vas in dat Ball,
Being arm'd from Top to Toe, Sir.

But 'twas by wise retreating,
When Orders were repeating,
    For when all's done,
    De Warld must own,
We had victorious beating.

For dey've lost twice our Men, Sir,
If you'll believe my Pen, Sir,
    And since a Wood
    Dos so much Good,
We'll ne'er fight on a Plain, Sir.

Four times we made 'em run, Sir,
And yet dey would come on, Sir,
    'Twas well deyr Foot
    Stood boldly to't,
Dey els had been undone, Sir.

Artagnan charm'd his Forces,
He lost one two tre Horses,
    De Duc de *Guich*
    Shot near de Breech,
Deserve Heroick Verses.

St. *George* in monstrous Passion,
Attack'd his rebel Nation,
    Begar *Mounsieur*,
    He hope next Year,
You'll make a new Invasion.

For do de Odds must be, Sir,
Vid us as all might see, Sir,
    Yet me have swore,
    Deyr Troops were more,
To infinite Degree, Sir.

                              Or

Or if you will make Peace, Sir,
For fear our Luck decrease, Sir,
    Dere ne'er was known,
    Since War begun,
So fit a time as dis, Sir.

All, all our Troops did Wonders,
And of more Martial Thunders,
    I'll write again,
    But now in Pain,
Leave off for fear of Blunders.

A Dialogue *Sung by a Boy and Girl, suppos'd a Brother and Sister. Set by Mr.* Akeroyd.

He.   AH ! my dearest, my dearest *Celide*,
          Tother Day I ask'd my Mother,
    Why thy Lodging chang'd must be,
    Why not still lye with thy Brother ;
She. I remember well you did,
    And I know too what she said,
    Lissis is a great Boy, great Boy grown,
    Therefore now must lye alone.

CHORUS.

He.   *To part us the Custom of Modesty votes,*
      Unless you had Breeches,
She. *Or you had long Coats.*

He.   I wonder what's in my little tiny Breeches,
    Sure there's some Witchcraft in the Stitches.
She. Or what Devil here resides,
    That my Petticoats thus hides,
    For I long for a Kiss,
He. So do I.

                                She.

She. Mother laughs an Hour or two, when I
    Sometimes ask to know why,
  A He and a She may not bed at our Size,
    As well as two Girls,
    Or as well as two Boys :
He. I will, since I am kept from you,
    Get a Wife as soon as may be ;
She. And I'll get a Husband too,
    Three times bigger than my Baby.

CHORUS.

*Let's laugh then, and follow our innocent Play,
And kiss when Mamma is gone out of the way ;
'Tis I fear we shall cry, when we know
For all that a Brother and Sister may do.*

The last Song *in the* Masque.   *Set by
Mr.* Courtivill.

CEase *Hymen*, cease thy Brow,
  Let Discord awe thou heavy Yoke,
Where Fools with trouble draw ;
I'm sworn Foe to all thy Law does bind,
Marriage from first Creation was design'd,
A Curse intail'd on wretched human kind.

Cease *Hymen*, cease thy Brow,
Let Discord awe ;
    'Tis noble Discord, gen'rous Strife,
    That gives the truest Tast of Life ;
Marriage first made Man fall,
    Had I been in the Garden plac'd,
    The Woman ne'er had made him tast,
'Twas foolish Loving damn'd us all.

A

A SONG.

A*Pelles* told the Painters fam'd in *Greece*,
　　To draw true Beauty was the hardest piece ;
And now, alass, the same defect we see
Descend, from Painting into Poetry :
Divine *Olympia's* Face no Skill can take,
　Each Feature does the feeble Artist blind,
And ah, what Muse a just Applause can make
　Of all the Charms in that Angelick kind.

Some are for pleasing Features far renown'd,
Others with Wit, or charming Voices wound ;
Many for Mein and Shape fond Lovers Prize,
And many make vast Conquests with their Eyes :
But ne'er were these Perfections found in one,
But in the fair *Olympia* alone ;
The fair *Olympia* Phænix-like appears,
A Wonder seen once in a Thousand Years.

[Second Movement.]

Then shew thy Power, great God of Love,
　That Laughs at Womans Craft ;
Make all her Charms less strongly move,
　And make her Heart more soft :
Ah, why should Beauty first ordain'd to please,
　　　Consume and Kill,
　　　And do such fatal Ill,
Since only she can cure, which causes the disease.

An ODE *on the Union of the King and Par-liament.   The Tune by Mr.* Jer. Clarke.

WHilst the *French* their Arms discover,
  By the Troops abroad they bring ;
We with Joy can send 'em over,
  Tidings that can make all *Europe* Ring :
English boys renown'd for warring,
  As Fame's glorious Records shew ;
Blest by Fate now leave off Jarring,
  And resolve to joyn 'gainst the common Foe :
No more frowning, *Batavians* think of drowning,
  But to *Spaniards* this jolly Ditty sing ;
England's Senate now agrees,
Cæsar can secure your Peace,
  Chant it at the Crowning ·
Of their Infant King.

Britain's Sons no danger fear,
  Whilst their Royal Fleet's well mann'd ;
Know tho' yet no Storms appearing,
  Peace is always best with the Sword in hand :
Honour's but an empty notion,
  As our plotting Neighbour shews ;
Breach of Faith may raise commotion,
  And in proper Season may come to blows :
Great five hundred, pray let us not be Plunder'd,
  Save our Lands then, and all unite at home ;
Guard the Crowns prerogative,
Boldly vote and nobly give,
  Then let any insolent Invader come.

A LAD *of the* Town.

A Lad o'th' Town thus made his moan,
  One Winter Morning early ;
Alas, that I must Lie alone,
  And *Moggy's* Bed so near me :
All Night I toss, I turn and sigh,
  Nor ever can I close my Eye ;
Thinking that I lig so nigh,
  The Lass I Love so dearly.

She's

She's all Delight from foot to crown,
  And just Eighteen her Age is;
And that she still must lie alone,
  My Heart and Soul inrages:
    I'd give the World I might put on
    Each Morn her Stocking or Shoon,
    If I were but her Serving Loon,
I'd never ask for Wages.

If *Moggey* would but be my Bride,
  I'd take no Parents warning;
Nor value all the World beside,
Nor any Lasses scorning:
    My Love is grown to such a height,
    I prize so much my own delight,
    I care not, had I her one Night,
If I were hang'd i'th' Morning.

To Chloris: *A* SONG.

IF my Addresses are grateful,
  Shew it in granting my Suit;
Or if my Passion be hateful,
  Leave me and end the dispute:
I hate your doubling and turning,
Like a cours'd Hare in a Morning;
Either comply as you should,
Or leave me to others that would.

A Scotch SONG *in the* Trick *for* Trick.

ABroad as I was walking, upon a Summer's day,
There I met a Beggar-woman cloathed all in Gray;
Her Cloaths they were so torn, you might have seen
    her Skin,
She was the first that taught me to see the Golin,
Ah, see the Golin my Jo! *see the Golin.*

You Youngsters of Delight, pray take it not in scorn,
She came of *Adam's* Seed, tho' she was basely born;
And tho' her Cloaths were torn, yet she had a Milk-
    white Skin,
    She was the first, &c.

She had a pretty little Foot, and a moist Hand,
With which she might compare to any Lady in the
    Land;
Ruby Lips, Cherry-cheeks, and a dimpled Chin,
    She was the first, &c.

When

When that Ay had wooed, and wad her twa my will,
Ay could not then devise the way to keep her Baby
     still ;
She bid me be at quiet, for she valued it not a pin,
  She was the first, &c.

Then she takes her Bearn up, and wraps it weel in
     cloaths,
And then she takes a Golin and stuck between her
     Toes ;
And ever as the Lurden cry'd, or made any din,
She shook her Foot, and cry'd my Jo, *see the Golin :*
And see the Golin, my Jo, *see the Golin.*

To CYNTHIA.

IF Beauty by Enjoyment can
     Reward a Love that's true,
To bless our Patience or our Pain,
     All I deserve from you.

But oh, to Love too well's a Curse,
     Of such a strange degree ;
Were my Fidelity far worse,
     Much happier should I be.

Sad Recompence, relentless Fate,
     To faithful Love does give ;
You're pleas'd in being obstinate,
     Whilst I in Tortures live.

Like wretches gull'd to Foreign Shores,
     I cruelly am serv'd ;
Instead of Loves dear promis'd Stores,
     Am made a Slave, and starv'd.

The

The *KING's Health : Set to* Farinel's *Ground.   In Six Parts.*

First Strain.

Second Strain.

Third Strain.

Fourth Strain.

Figg.
The Sixth Strain.

The First Strain.

JOY to Great *Cæsar*,
   Long Life, Love and Pleasure;
'Tis a Health that Divine is,
Fill the Bowl high as mine is:
   Let none fear a Feaver,
But take it off thus Boys;
   Let the King Live for ever,
'Tis no matter for us Boys.

The Second Strain.

   Try all the Loyal,
   Defy all,
   Give denyall;
Sure none thinks his Glass too big here,
   Nor any *Prig* here,
   Or Sneaking *Whig* here,
   Of Cripple *Tony's* Crew,
   That now looks blue,
   His Heart akes too,
   The *Tap* won't do,
   His Zeal so true,
   And Projects new,
   Ill Fate does now pursue.

The Third Strain.

   Let *TORIES* Guard the King,
   Let *Whigs* in Halters swing;
   Let *Pilk* and *Shute* be sham'd,
   Let Bugg'ring *Oats* be damn'd:
   Let Cheating *Player* be Nick'd,
   The turn-coat Scribe be Kick'd;
   Let Rebel City Dons,
   Ne'er beget their Sons:
   Let ev'ry *Wiggish* Peer,
   That Rapes a Lady fair,
   And leaves his only Dear,
   The Sheets to gnaw and tear,

Be

Be punish'd out of hand,
And forc'd to pawn his Land
T' attone the grand Affair.

The Fourth Strain.

Great *CHARLES*, like *Jehovah*,
   Spares those would Un-King Him ;
And warms with his Graces,
   The Vipers that sting Him :
Till Crown'd with just Anger,
   The Rebel he Seizes ;
Thus Heaven can Thunder,
   When ever it pleases.

Jigg.

Then to the *Duke* fill, fill up the Glass,
The Son of our *Martyr*, belov'd of the King ;
   Envy'd and Lov'd,
   Yet blest from above,
Secur'd by an Angel safe under his Wing.

The Sixth Strain.

Faction and Folly,
And State Melancholy, .
With *Tony* in *Whigland* for ever shall dwell ;
   Let Wit, Wine, and Beauty,
   Then teach us our Duty,
For none e'er can Love, or be Wise and Rebel.

A Royal ODE, *Congratulating the Happy Accession to the Crown, and Coronation of our most Gracious Soveraign Lady Queen* ANN.   *The Words in Imitation of the foregoing* SONG, *and fitted to some Strains of the same Ground.*

M A R S now is Arming,
  The War comes on Storming ;
All *Europe* is viewing,
What *England* is doing :
The slighted (1) Memorial,   (1) *The* French
In *France* and th' *Escurial,*   *Memorial.*
Has baulk'd (2) Gallick *Nero,*   (2) *The* French *K.*
And *Porto* (3) *Carero ;*   (3) *The new K. of*
Britains cease weeping,   Spain's *chief Min.*
For (4) *Pan* that lies sleeping ;   (4) *King* Will.
Tho' *Jove* us denies him,
Yet (5) *Pallas* supplies him.   (5) *Q.* Ann.
Then Sing out ye Muses,
What *Phœbus* infuses ;
Divine is the occasion,
Queen *ANN's* Coronation.

The Second Strain.

Pair your Hearts and joyn,
For now the Rightful Line
Has left you no Excuse,
For Jarring or abuse :
The thought of Right and Wrong,
That plagu'd ye all so long ;
No more be now let in,
To raise the *Senate's* Spleen :
Nor simple Feuds let grow,
'Twixt the *High-Church* and the *Low ;*

But

But all resolve to go,
To one at least for show :
And then made happy so,
Direct your Anger's blow ;
Against the Common Foe.

The Third Strain.

Divine *Gloriana,*
    Now Rules the glad Nation ;
Mild, Prudent, and Pious,
    Without Affectation :
Sence, Justice, and Pity,
    Her Life still renewing ;
And Queen of all Hearts,
E'er the Pageant of Crowning.

The Fourth Strain.

All the Radiant Court of Heaven have blest Her,
Bright *Astrea* leaves the Sky to assist Her ;
Whilst on her from all,
    Revolves the Sacred praise,
    Of fam'd *Eliza's* Days.

*Sing then ye Muses,
What* Phœbus *infuses ;
Divine is the Occasion,
Queen* ANN's *Coronation.*

This *Chorus* may be sung to the Ground-Bass.

The Scotch *Lasses* SONG.

WAe is me, what ails our Northern Loons,
    That with jangling make the Times so baddy,
Snarling like a breed of hungry Hounds,
    Welladay, they must be aw drunk or maddy ;
        But tho' Peace they destroy,
        I have still some Joy,
    Since I wed a bonny young Highland Laddy.

London's wily Lads are all at Strife,
    High and Low Boys daily new Fears are bringing,
Whilst there they lead a woful Life,
    In a Meadow *Jockey* and I sit singing ;
        A sweet Hornpipe he plays
        To my Roundelays,
    Whilst the merry *Edenbrough* Bells are ringing.

See the Daizy, and the gay Primrose,
    Merry Spring is coming to make us gladdy,
Winter's vanish'd with its Frost and Snows,
And no Storm will gar me to be saddy,
        For when the Wind blows,
        Jockey wraps me close,
From the Cold within his Highland pladdy.

Who would pine to have high place at Court,
    Out, away, 'tis but a fleeting Vision,
Who would leave the Jolly Country Sport,
For the Gown or Sword Man's gay Condition ;
        Give me ten Mark a Year,
        And my Highland dear,
And adieu to Pride, and all Ambition.

The Crafty Mistriss's Resolution.

ALL the Town so lewd are grown,
   Hereafter you must excuse me ;
If when you discover your self a Lover,
  I think it is all a Lye ;
Oaths and Sighs, and melting Eyes,
  You'll sacrifice to seduce me,
The silly poor Women are often undone,
  And happily warn'd am I.

Excuse me for flying, and for denying,
  For Faith, Sir, I must refuse you,
Excuse me for knowing the Cheats of your Wooing,
  And for the Request excuse me :
Excuse me if when you vow'd and swore,
  I thought you design'd to deceive me ;
But now who makes Love 'till his Eyes run o'er,
  Shall never hereafter abuse me.

Wit and Youth did once invade
  My Heart, e'er I was twenty,
And I silly Creature, thro' meer good Nature,
  Believ'd him what e'er he swore.
Young, and unpractis'd in the Trade
  Of Love, I was not scanty ;
But he who my Innocence then betray'd,
  Shall never deceive me more.

For now tho' he flatter, and ogle and chatter,
  And still in the Dance will chuse me,
Then argue the Case too, and look like an Ass too,
  He after all this shall lose me :
For now I will Female-Cunning use,
  And all our stock of Revenge produce,
The Rebel to Honour has broke the Truce,
  And all Mankind shall excuse me.

His soft Words I will not mind,
  Wherewith he strives to amuse me ;
Nor to his feign'd Passion, so much in Fashion,
  Will I at all give heed.

Tho' with Sighs he swares he dies,
  And vows he can't live if he lose me,
Yet to his Tale I'll be deaf as the Wind,
  And never will let him speed.

And by my so doing, I'll fit him for wooing,
  With an intent to abuse me :
He that wou'd not marry, I'faith now shall tarry,
  And for not yielding, excuse me :
By Man, I'll be decoy'd no more,
  My Passion no more it undoes me :
Once I believed what the false one had swore,
  But yet for all that, he shall lose me.

Tho' Wit and Youth they do plead,
  And with new Charms present me,
And tho' he flatter, he's never the better,
  For I'll believe him no more :
No more to Love I'll be betray'd,
  But shun the Danger it meant me,
'Tis happier far for to live a Maid,
  If there were no more Men in store.

But since there are many, and I can have any,
  Whose Honesty will not abuse me,
I'll find one that's true to, and so bid adieu to
  The Man that could once refuse me :
'Twas at my Honour it seems you aim'd,
  But your Intent too soon you proclaim'd,
For which by the Virtuous you must be blam'd,
  Whilst all Mankind shall excuse me.

The

*The Jolly Toper, that wont leave his Bottle
to get the best Wife in Christendom.*

The TOPER.

P Rattles and Tattles,
       O'er Bottles,
Shall still cherish my Fancy,
   Better, and sweeter,
       And greater,
Than dull Tea with *Nancy.*
She has forbid me Wine,
   Or else she'll not marry,
But were she all Divine,
   A Maid she should tarry ;
Flouts, and Lowers, and Frowns,
   Cross Wives thus e'ery Day mingle,
Wine that Care confounds,
   We share that are single.

Harry and *Jerry*
       The merry,
Are both Boys of good Mettle.
   Sprightly and tightly,
       And nightly,
The whole Nation we settle.
Nancy ne'er hurts my Brain,
   No wishing, nor hoping,
Tho' she now thinks to raign,
   And hinder my toping,
Says, whene'er I ask,
   A Sot will never be civil,
Boy bring tother Flask,
   And let her go to the Devil.

                         The

The Politick CLUB.

A Country Bumpkin that Trees did grub,
  A Vicar that us'd the Pulpit to drub,
And two or three more o'er a Stoop of strong Bub,
      Late met on a Jolly Occasion.
No ill Contrivance to cheat or rob,
But each in his turn, to speak a dry Bob,
As drunk as five Lords, and as poor as *Job*,
      Thus settl'd the State of the Nation.

Farmer. Oh Neighbour, Neighbour, what times are
    these?
How long will't be e'er we shall have Peace,
My Coat's out at Elbows, my Breeches at Knees,
    Oh, *England*, thou art a sweet Nation.
The *Mounsieur* goes on in his former way,
The Troops are ready without their Pay,
To stare on each other in Battle Array.
    Oh, *England*, thou art a sweet Nation.

Vicar. The Mob have been to Religion true,
Pull'd down the Red, and set up the Blew:
They have done their best, give the Devil his due,
    With a Protestant active Endeavour.
Lawyer. And what no Nation before did dare,
The Coin is chang'd in a time of War,
Which shews we have Bullion enough and to spare.
    Oh, would it may prove so for ever.

Citizen. And tho' Bank Bills we've discounted found,
And that for a Hundred, we've got but five Pound,
'Tis mill'd, and its pretty, it shines, and it's round.
    Oh, *England*, thou art a sweet Nation.
The Clippers Trading is at an end,
I wish it may our Condition mend,
They've no Coin to clip now, nor we none to spend.
    Oh, *England*, thou art a sweet Nation.

Courtier. The King his Taxes no Friend can grutch,
Tho' Jacobites bawl that we lavish too much;
That all runs away to the *French* and the *Dutch*.
    And nothing is left more to drein Boys.
        Citiz.

Citiz. But let us look within our Doors,
How Backs and Bellies exhaust our Stores,
Let's take up our Wives, & let's take down our
    Whores.
            We've enough for another Campaign Boys.

Courtier. Tho' Cits cry out that they are undone,
A Cuckold's Profit can ne'er be gone ;
Their Wives are well rigg'd, and gold Laces still on.
            Oh, *England*, thou art a sweet Nation.
Lawyer. Tho' Goldsmith's break too, and shut up Door,
'Tis more to cheat ye, than want of Ore,
For Rogues will be Rogues, whether wealthy or poor.
            Oh, *England*, thou art a sweet Nation.

Citizen. Great Joy will come from the Chequer Board,
When true Effects all our Tallies afford,
Court. And all our new Medals come out of their Hoard.
            That, that will be great Consolation.

Vicar. When each Man's Purse to our Party leans,
And Senates study right ways and means,
Farmer. And large Sums of Gold comes from Bishops
    and Deans.
            Then, then will be true Reformation.

Lawyer. Tho' foreign Gamesters our Ruin plot,
And in our Tables perceive a Blot,
We'll win the Game afterwards, with a why not.
            Oh, *England*, thou art a sweet Nation.
Poor *Britain's* Troubles then soon relieve,
And in our stead, make our Enemies grieve,
The Peace will be settl'd, the Muses will live.
            Oh, *England*, thou art a sweet Nation.

The

The Farmer's Daughter: A SONG.

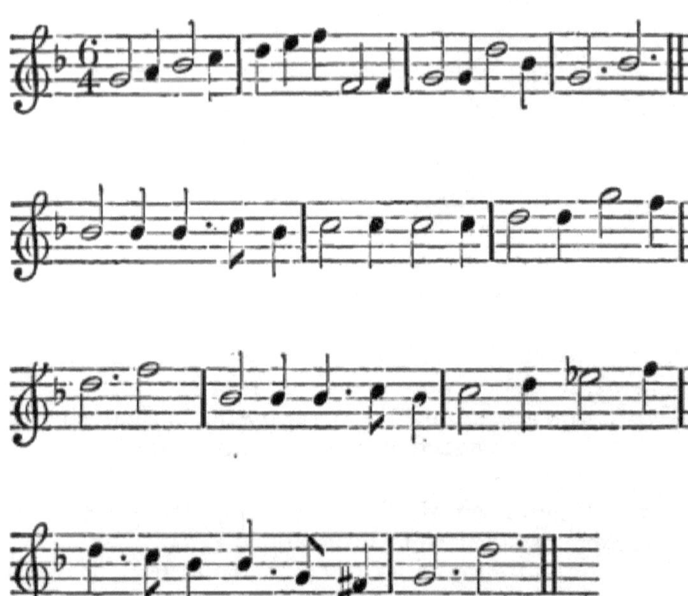

COLD and Raw the North did blow,
   Bleak in the Morning early;
All the Trees were hid in Snow,
   Dagl'd by Winter yearly:
When come Riding over a Knough,
   I met with a Farmer's Daughter;
Rosie Cheeks and bonny Brow,
   Good faith made my Mouth to water.

Down I vail'd my Bonnet low,
   Meaning to shew my breeding;
She return'd a graceful bow,
   A Visage far exceeding:

I

I ask'd her where she went so soon,
    And long'd to begin a Parly ;
She told me unto the next Market Town,
    A purpose to sell her Barly.

In this purse, sweet Soul, said I,
    Twenty pounds lie fairly ;
Seek no farther one to buy,
    For I'se take all thy Barly :
Twenty more shall buy Delight,
    Thy Person I Love so dearly ;
If thou wouldst stay with me all Night,
    And go home in the Morning early.

If Twenty pound could buy the Globe,
    Quoth she, this I'd not do, Sir ;
Or were my Kin as poor as *Job*,
    I wo'd not raise 'em so, Sir :
For should I be to Night your friend,
    We'st get a young Kid together ;
And you'd be gone ere the nine Months end,
    And where should I find a Father ?

I told her I had Wedded been,
    Fourteen years and longer ;
Or else I'd choose her for my Queen,
    And tie the Knot much stronger :
She bid me then no farther rome,
    But manage my Wedlock fairly ;
And keep Purse for poor Spouse at home,
    For some other shall have her Barly.

A

A little of one with t'other ; A New Song,
to the Scotch *Tune of* Cold *and* Raw.

A *Beau* dress'd fine met *Miss* divine,
  Resolv'd to Court and wooe her,
With Kiss and Hat, yet she all that
  Thought little good could do her :
She gave a Frown, but would not own
  His Love for all that pother ;
Her Brain did soar at something more,
  A little of one with t'other.

You may Sir skip my Hand and Lip,
  That bear your idle Kissing ;
Your Barren suit will yield no Fruit,
  If something else be missing :
I wont dispute, you may Salute
  Your Sister, or your Mother ;
But who'll refine his Joys, must joyn
  A little of one with t'other.

To cheat me thus like *Tantalus*,
  It makes me Pine with Plenty ;
With shadows store, and nothing more,
  Your Substance is too dainty :
A flow'ry Tree is like to thee,
  And but a blooming Lover ;
Flowers get Fruit, or else be mute,
  A little of one with t'other.

Sharp joyn'd with Flat, there's Mirth in that,
  A low Note and a higher ;
The Alt and Mean, with Fuge between,
  Such Musick we desire :
All of one String does loathing bring,
  Change is good Musick's Mother,
Then leave my Face, and sound my Bass,
  A little of one with t'other.

No warmth desire without a Fire,
  No bargain without Writing;
In Rapture then clap too your Pen,
  You were before Inditing:
And if I take the Lines you make,
  As from a willing Lover;
Like Lawyers deal, first Write, then Seal
  A little of one with t'other.

No greater truth cou'd warm the Youth,
  The Lady's Breath was rosie;
He laid her down on flow'ry ground,
  To treat her with a Poesie:
And whilst in hast he claspt her fast,
  And did with Kisses smother,
She cry'd my Heaven, your sweetly given,
  A little of one with t'other.

A SONG.

M AKE your Honour Miss, *tholl loll, loll,*
Now to me Child, *tholl loll, loll,*
Airy and easie now, *tholl loll, loll,*
Very well done Miss, *tholl loll, loll,*
Raise up your Body Child, *tholl loll, loll,*
Then you in time will Rise, *hoh, tholl la.*

Hold up your Head Miss, *tholl loll, loll,*
Wipe your Nose Child, *tholl loll,*
When I press on ye, *tholl loll, loll,*
Fall back easie Miss, *tholl loll, loll,*
Keep out your Toes too, *tholl loll, loll,*
Then you'll learn presently, *hoh, tholl la.*

Bear your Hips swimmingly, *tholl loll, loll,*
Keep your Eyes languishing, *tholl loll, loll,*
Z—— where's your Ears now ? *tholl loll, loll,*
Leave off your Jerking, *tholl loll, loll,*
Keep your Knees open, *tholl loll, loll,*
Else you will never do, *hoh, tholl la.*

If you will Love me Miss, *tholl loll, loll, loll,*
You shall Dance rarely Child, *tholl loll, loll,*
You are a Fortune Miss, *tholl loll, loll,*
And must be Married Child, *tholl loll, loll,*
Give me your Money Miss, *tholl loll, loll,*
Then I will give you my *hoh, tholl la.*

A SONG.

OF noble Race was *Shinking,*
 The Line of *Owen Tudor,*
Thum, thum, thum, thum,
But her Renown is fled and gone,
 Since cruel Love pursu'd her.

Fair *Winnies* Eyes bright shining,
 And Lilly Breasts alluring ;
Poor *Jenkins* Heart with fatal Dart,
 Have wounded past all curing.

Her was the prettiest fellow,
 At Foot-ball or at Cricket ;
At Hunting Chace, or nimble Race,
 Cots-plut how her cou'd prick it.

But now all Joys are flying,
 All Pale and wan her Cheeks too,
Her Heart so akes, her quite forsakes,
 Her Herrings and her Leeks too.

No more must dear Metheglin,
 Be top'd at good *Montgomery ;*
And if Love sore, smart one week more,
 Adieu Creem-Cheese and Flomery.

A

A SONG.

Orc'd by a Cruel lawless Fate,
    I lov'd a Nymph with Passion ;
But found alas, I came too late
    To sway her Inclination :
Her Heart was given a Coxcomb's fee,
    Whose Face had Introduc'd him ;
Though not one grain of Sence had he,
    To know how well she us'd him.

I try'd if worth could make her kind,
    And hourly made advances ;
But who can e'er the Charm unbind,
    In Womans stubborn Fancies :
I calmly did her foible shew,
    Where e'er he came, abus'd him ;
I call'd him Fool, I prov'd him so,
    Yet she the better us'd him.

I hate, she cry'd, your God of Wit,
    Our Sex should all oppose him ;
'Tis he that Charms my Appetite,
    Shall sleep upon my Bosom :
This senseless stuff my Love withdrew,
    And cur'd my Melancholy ;
I kick'd her Brute, then bid adieu,
    To every Female folly.

A

A SONG ; *on a Lady's going into the* Bath.

WHEN *Sylvia* in Bathing, her Charms does expose,
The pretty Banquet dancing under her Nose;
My Heart is just ready to part from my Soul,
And leap from the Ga——'ry into the Bowl:
　　Each day I provide too,
　　A bribe for her Guide too,
　　And gave her a Crown,
To bring me the Water where she sat down;
Let crazy Physitians think Pumping a Cure,
That Virtue is doubtful, but *Sylvia's* is sure.

The Fidlers I hire to play something Sublime,
And all the while throbbing my Heart beats the Time;
She enters, they Flourish, and cease when she goes,
That who it is address'd to, straight ev'ry one knows;
　　Wou'd I were a Vermin,
　　Call'd one of her Chairmen,
　　Or serv'd as a Guide;
Tho' show'd as they do a damn'd tawny Hide,
Or else like a Pebble at bottom cou'd lye,
To Ogle her Beauties, how happy were I.

A

A SONG.

UPON a sunshine Summers day,
  When every Tree was green and gay ;
The Morning blusht with *Phœbus* ray,
Just then ascending from the Sea :
As *Silvia* did a Hunting ride,
A lovely Cottage he espy'd ;
Where lovely *Cloe* Spinning sat,
And still she turn'd her Wheel about.

Her Face a Thousand Graces crown,
Her curling Hair was lovely brown ;
Her rowling Eyes all Hearts did win,
And white as Down of Swans her Skin:

So

So taking her plain Dress appears,
Her Age not passing Sixteen Years ;
The Swain lay sighing at her Foot,
Yet still she turn'd her Wheel about.

Thou sweetest of thy tender kind,
Cries he, this ne'er can suit thy Mind ;
Such Grace attracting noble Loves,
Was ne'er design'd for Woods and Groves :
Come, come with me, to Court my Dear,
Partake my Love and Honour there ;
And leave this Rural sordid rout,
And turn no more thy Wheel about.

At this with some few Modest sighs.
She turns to him her Charming Eyes ;
Ah ! tempt me Sir, no more she cries,
Nor seek my Weakness to surprise :
I know your Art's to be believ'd,
I know how Virgins are deceiv'd ;
Then let me thus my Life wear out,
And turn my harmless Wheel about.

By that dear panting Breast cries he,
And yet unseen divinity ;
Nay, by my Soul that rests in thee,
I swear this cannot, must not be :
Ah ! cause not my eternal woe,
Nor kill the Man that Loves thee so ;
But go with me, and ease my doubt,
And turn no more thy Wheel about.

His cunning Tongue so play'd its part,
He gain'd admission to her Heart ;
And now she thinks it is no Sin,
To take Loves fatal poison in :
But ah ! too late she found her fault,
For he her Charms had soon forgot ;
And left her e'er the Year ran out,
In Tears to turn her Wheel about.

A SONG, *to a Ground of Dr.* John Blow's.

S Tubborn Church-division,
   Folly and Ambition,
  Caus'd with great Derision,
  Poor *England's* sad condition ;
Princes leave their Stations, by strange Abdications :
   New ones come to ease us,
   Yet nothing e'er can please us,
Happy's the Man then that shuns the Great,
That pleaseth himself in a Rural State.

   With ease and in a sweet retreat,
     Avoids all Jarrs and Faction,
     In his small Dominions,
     Vents no false Opinions,
Nor deserts the true, for *Papist,* or *Socinian :*
  But sits down with his Friends around,
     Whilst the Glass is crown'd,
     And the Healths abound,
To the King and the Queen the best in the Town.

     The Fleet or Armies Action,
     Argues still with reason,
     Speaks nor hears no Treason ;
     Nor Arraigns the Sence,
  Of five Hundred Heads to please one :
     Plaintiff or Defendants,
     Ne'er get his attendance,
He wishes well to all, that are at *White-Hall,*
  But he Loves no Court dependance.

     Books admires when Witty,
     Good Musick and a Ditty,
  And takes a Spouse, to adorn his House,
     That's Rich and kind, and pretty ;
Merry, merry, merrily discards all sorrow,
Warily does never, never lend nor borrow,
  Generously entertains his Friends to day,
And is the same to Morrow.

The

The Moderator's *Dream; in an Harangue between the Ghost of Queen* BESSE, *and the* Genius *of* GREAT BRITAIN : *Occasioned by the Disappointment of the Burning the* Pope, *and the Mobb's Procession on the* 17th *of* November. *The Words made to a pretty Tune, call'd* Chimney Sweep.

WHEN *Soll* to *Thetis* Pool,
 Save the Queen, save the Queen,
Rode down his Head to cool,
 Save the Queen :
Close by a purling Stream,
That might give a Poet Theam ;
I Slept, and had a Dream,
 Save the Queen, save the Queen.

Methought Queen *BESSE* arose,
 Save the Queen, &c.
From Mansion of Repose,
 Save the Queen :
The *Genius* of our Land
Came in too at her command,
And thus Harangue maintain'd,
 Save the Queen, &c.

Genius.

What mean you, awful Shade,
 Save the Queen, &c.
When such Results are made ?
 Save the Queen :
When Concord is confest,
And comes Post from East to West,
What makes you leave your Rest ?
 Save the Queen, &c.

The

The Queen's Speech.

The Sovereign then reply'd,
   Save the Queen, save the Queen,
E'er since the time I dy'd,
   Save the Queen:
My Praise aloft did mount,
Till now late on strange Account,
I've had a vile Affront;
   Save the Queen, &c.

The Day of high Renown,
   Save the Queen, &c.
That long my Fame did Crown,
   Save the Queen;
My Friends old *Rome* to shame,
A most glorious show did Frame,
In Honour of my Name;
   Save the Queen, &c.

A *Pope* did Gay appear,
   Save the Queen, &c.
St. *George* was likewise there,
   Save the Queen:
A Dev'l of graceful Size,
Like himself without disguise,
Stood by to give Advice;
   Save the Queen, &c.

Four Cardinals in Caps,
   Save the Queen, &c.
Four Monks with bloated Chaps,
   Save the Queen:
Four Capuchines in Bays,
And to make the People gaze,
Two Hundred Lights to blaze;
   Save the Queen, &c.

But when 'twas to be shown,
   Save the Queen, &c.
In Splendour o're the Town,
   Save the Queen, &c.

A

A Troop of Grenadiers,
Put 'em all in Panick Fears,
By Order of some P——s ;
  Save the Queen, save the Queen.

They Seiz'd my Puppets all,
  Save the Queen, &c.
And bore 'em to *Whitehall,*
  Save the Queen, &c.
St. *George,* who look'd so great,
With the *Pope* and Dev'l his Mate,
Were Pris'ners made of State ;
  Save the Queen, &c.

My Glory thus they Cloud,
  Save the Queen, &c.
And disoblige my Croud,
  Save the Queen :
Who would have shewn that Night,
By the Power of Zealous might,
A Cause most pure and bright ;
  Save the Queen, &c.

But Property must be,
  Save the Queen, &c.
Allow'd in each Degree,
  Save the Queen :
And some were there that saw,
Who have sworn to mend this flaw,
By force of Common Law ;
  Save the Queen, &c.

A P——r of Noble Hope,
  Save the Queen, &c.
Lays Claim unto the *Pope,*
  Save the Queen :
A Doctor of Esteem,
And Religious to the brim,
Swears Dev'l belongs to him,
  Save the Queen, &c.

A

A Female W————g in Town,
   Save the Queen, &c.
Does the Pretender own,
   Save the Queen :
She says his Coat was gay,
And since thus 'tis took away,
The Government shall pay ;
   Save the Queen, &c.

Great Reason too they have,
   Save the Queen, &c.
Some think, whose Heads are Grave,
   Save the Queen :
Since all that was aim'd at,
Was to shew a Mob as great,
As High-Boys did of late ;
   Save the Queen.

The Genius *Answers.*

The *Genius* Answer made,
   Save the Queen, &c.
With Reverence to your Shade,
   Save the Queen :
When Mobs in Tumult swell,
'Tis the same as Fiends in Hell,
Remember * *Massinell ;*
   Save the Queen, &c.

The *Tory* Mob that's past,
   Save the Queen, &c.
Were timely well supprest,
   Save the Queen :
You Cits the Guards may thank,
For had one day more grown rank,
Reform'd had been your Bank ;
   Save the Queen, &c.

A People train'd to Grace,
   Save the, &c.
Deserve undoubted Praise,
   Save the Queen :

* A Fisherman of *Naples*, that in five days Time rais'd such a Mob, that he Insulted the Viceroy and Nobles, and overturned the whole Government.

But

But Morals that belong
(I must Question) to a Throng,
Two Hundred Thousand strong ;
    Save the Queen, &c.

Methinks I see 'em meet,
    Save the, &c.
And fill up *Lombard-street,*
    Save the, &c.
Each Banker standing bare,
That his Bags they will not spare,
An Ague has for fear ;
    Save the Queen, &c.

A Noble Lord at home,
    Save the, &c.
Saluting Captain *Tom,*
    Save the, &c.
Half melted with his fears,
Forc'd to Treat in Elbow Chairs,
A Rabble rout of Bears ;
    Save the Queen, &c.

This was the Case we read,
    Save the, &c.
With * *Tyler* and *Jack Cade,*   * Two Notorious
    Save the, &c.   Rebels, that raised
And might as well be so,   prodigious Tumults
Had you made Procession now,   in *England.*
And gone on with your show ;
    Save the Queen, &c.

Not that there's real Fear,
    Save the, &c.
Of Mobs whilst I am here,
    Save the, &c.
But still where Reason rules,
The old Proverb wisely Schools,
No Jesting with Edge Tools ;
    Save the Queen, &c.

Let

Let Moderation guide,
   Save the Queen, save the Queen;
And lay such Jests aside,
   Save the Queen:
For Trivial things like these,
Oft make fatal Feuds Increase,
And are no Friends to Peace,
   Save the Queen, save the Queen.

Let then the Scarlet Whore,
   Save the, &c.
In Rags burn as before,
   Save the, &c.
Let Satan close his Jaws,
And for the Pretender's Ca
Let's leave it to our Laws,
   Save the, &c.

And so Majestick Spright,
   Save the, &c.
I bid your Grace good Night,
   Save the Queen:
I've now no more remains,
But to cease Poetick Pains,
And guard the *Saint* that Reigns,
   Save the Queen, save the Queen.

A

A SONG.

B OAST no more fond Love, thy Power,
    Mingling Passions sweet and sower;
Bow to *Cælia*, show thy Duty,
Cælia sways the World of Beauty:
Venus now must kneel before her,
And admiring Crowds adore her.

Like the Sun that gilds the Morning,
Cælia shines, but more adorning;

She

She like Fate, can wound a Lover,
Goddess like too, can recover.:
She can Kill, or save from dying,
The Transported Soul is flying.

Sweeter than the blooming Rose is,
Whiter than the falling Snow is ;
Then such Eyes the Great Creator
Chose his Lamps to kindle Nature ;
Curst is he that can refuse her,
    Ah, hard Fate, that I must loose her.

Brother Solon's *Hunting* SONG.   *Sung by Mr.* Dogget.

TAntivee, tivee, tivee, tivee, High and Low,
    Hark, hark how the Merry, merry Horn does
  blow,
As through the Lanes and Meadows we go,
  As Puss has run over the Down ;
When Ringwood and Rockwood, and Jowler & Spring,
And Thunder and Wonder made all the Woods ring,
And Horsmen and Footmen, hey ding, a ding ding,
  Who envies the Pleasure and State of a Crown.

Then follow, follow, follow, follow Jolly boys,
Keep in with the Beagles now whilst the Scent lies,
The fiery Fac'd God is just ready to rise,
  Whose Beams all our Pleasure controuls ;
Whilst over the Mountains and Valleys we rowl,
And *Wat's* fatal Knell in each hollow we toll ;
And in the next Cottage tope off a full Bowl,
  What Pleasure like Hunting can cherish the Soul.

A

A SONG *Representing the going of a* Pad.

WHEN for Air
I take my Mare,
And mount her first,
Walk.   She walks just thus,
Her Head held low,
And Motion slow;
With Nodding, Plodding,
Wagging, Jogging,
Dashing, Plashing,
Snorting, Starting,
Whimsically she goes:
Then Whip stirs up,
Trot.   Trot, Trot, Trot;
Ambling then with easy slight,
Pace.   She riggles like a Bride at Night;
Her shuffling hitch,
Regales my Britch;
Trott.   Whilst Trott, Trott, Trott, Trott,
Brings on the Gallop,
Gallop.   The Gallop, the Gallop,
The Gallop, and then a short
Trott.   Trott, Trott, Trott, Trott,
Straight again up and down,
Gallop.   Up and down, up and down,
Till she comes home with a Trott,
Trott.   When Night dark grows.

Just

Just so *Phillis,*
Fair as Lillies,
Walk.   As her Face is,
Has her Paces ;
And in Bed too,
Like my Pad too ;
Nodding, Plodding,
Wagging, Jogging,
Dashing, Plashing,
Flirting, Spirting,
Artful are all her ways :
Trott.   Heart thumps pitt, patt,
Trott, Trott, Trott, Trott :
Pace.   Ambling, then her Tongue gets loose,
Whilst wrigling near I press more close :
Ye Devil she crys,
I'll tear your Eyes,
Trott.   When Main seiz'd,
Bum squeez'd,
Gallop. I Gallop, I Gallop, I Gallop, I Gallop,
Trott.   And Trott, Trott, Trott, Trott,
Streight again up and down,
Gallop. Up and down, up and down,
Till the last Jerk with a Trott,
Trott.   Ends our Love Chase.

A DIALOGUE *between a Town Spark and his Miss.*

She. DID you not promise me when you lay by me,
  That you would marry me, can you deny me?
He. If I did promise thee, 'twas but to try thee,
  Call up your Witnesses, else I defie thee.

She. Ah, who would trust you men that swear and vow
   so,
  Born only to deceive, how can you do so?
He. If we can swear and lye, you can dissemble,
  And then to hear the Lye, would make one
   tremble.
She. Had I not lov'd, you had found a Denial,
  My tender Heart, alas, was but too real;
He. Should a new Shower encrease the Flood,
  Too soon would overflow.

He. Real I know you were, I've often try'd ye,
  Real to forty more Lovers besides me.
She. If thousands lov'd me, where was my Trans-
   gression,
  You were the only He, e'er got Possession?
He. Thou could'st talk prettily, e'er thou could'st go
   Child;
  But I'm too old and wise to be sham'd so, Child.
She. Tho' y'are so cruel you'll never believe me,
  Yet do but take the Child, all I forgive thee.
He. Send your *Kid* home to me, I will take care on't,
  If't has the Mother's Gifts, 'twill prove a rare one.

Willey's *Intreague: A New* SONG.

'TWAS when Summer was Rosie,
   In Woods and Fields many a Poesie ;
When late young Flaxen-hair'd *Nelly*,
Was way-ly'd by bonny black *Willey :*
He Oagled her, and Teiz'd her,
He Smuggled her, and Squeez'd her,
  He Grabbled her too very near the Belly ;
She cry'd I never will hear ye,
Oh Lord ! oh Lord ! I can't bear ye,
  Ye tickle, tickle so, tickle, tickle so *Willey*.

Soon the fit tho' was over,
And *Nelly* her Breath did recover ;
When *Willey* bated his Wooing,
And cooly prepared to be going :
When *Nelly* tho' he teiz'd her,
And Grabbled her and Squeez'd her,
Cry'd, stay a little, I vow and swear I could kill ye,
Another touch I can bear ye,
Oh Lord ! oh Lord ! I will hear ye,
Then tickle me again, tickle me again, *Willey*.

    The

The SERENADE,

A SONG *in the Injur'd Princess or a Fatal Wager, Set by* Colonel Pack.

THE Larks awake the drowzy morn,
  My dearest lovely *Chloe* rise,
And with thy dazling Rays adorn,
  The ample World and Azure Skies :
Each Eye of thine out-shines the Sun,
  Tho' deck'd in all his Light ;
As much as he excells the Moon,
Or each small twinkling Star at Noon,
  Or Meteor of the Night.

Look down and see your Beauty's power,
  See, see the Heart in which you reign ;
No Conquer'd Slave in Triumph bore,
  Did ever wear so strong a Chain :
Feed me with Smiles that I may Live,
  I'll ne'er wish to be free ;
Nor ever hope for kind Reprieve,
Or Loves grateful bondage leave,
  For Immortality.

A SONG.

WHY are my Eyes still flowing,
  Why do my Heart thus trembling move?
Why do I sigh when going
  To see the darling Saint I Love?
Ah! she's my Heaven, and in her Eyes the Deity;
There is no Life like what she can give,
Nor any Death like taking my leave:
  Tell me no more of Glory,
To Court's Ambition I've resign'd;
  But tell a long, long story,
Of *Celia's* Face, her Shape and Mind;
Speak too of Raptures, that wou'd Life destroy to enjoy:
Had I a Diadem, Scepter and Ball,
For one happy Minute I'd part with them all.

A *New* Scotch SONG.

WAlking down the Highland Town,
    There I saw Lasses many ;
But upon the Bank in the highest Rank,
    Was one more gay than any :
I Look'd about for one kind Face,
    And I saw *Billy Scrogy ;*
I ask'd of him what was her Name,
    They call'd her *Catherine Logy.*

I travelled East, and I travelled West,
    And I travelled through *Strabogy ;*
But the fairest Lass that e'er I see,
    Was pretty *Catherine Logy.*

I Travelled East, and I Travelled West,
    And Travel'd through *Strabogy ;*
But I'd watch a long Winters Night,
    To see fair *Catherine Logy.*

I've a Love in *Lamer Moor,*
    A dainty Love in *Leith,* Sir ;
And another Love in *Edinborough,*
    And twa Loves in *Dalkeith,* Sir.

Ride I East, or Ride I West,
    My Love She's still before me,
But gin my Wife shou'd ken aw this,
    I shou'd be very sorry.

The

The Scotch *Parson's Daughter.*

P*EGGY* in Devotion,
     Bred from tender Years ;
From my Loving motion,
     Still was call'd to Prayers :
I made muckle bustle,
     Love's dear Fort to win ;
But the Kirk Apostle,
     Told her 'twas a Sin.

Fasting

Fasting and Repentance,
  And such Whining Cant;
With the Dooms-day sentence,
  Frighted my young Saint:
He taught her the Duty,
  Heavenly joys to know;
I that lik'd her Beauty,
  Taught her those below.

Nature took my part still,
  Sence did Reason blind;
That for all his Art still,
  She to me inclin'd:
Strange delight hereafter,
  Did so dull appear;
She as I had taught her,
  Vow'd to share 'em here.

Faith 'tis worth your Laughter,
  'Mongst the canting Race;
Neither Son nor Daughter,
  Ever yet had Grace:
Peggy on the Sunday,
  With her Daddy vext;
Came to me on Monday,
  And forgot his Text.

The

The BLACKBIRD : *A New* SONG.

R Oom, room, room for a Rover,
　　Yonder Town's so hot ;
I a Country Lover
　　Bless my Freedom got :
This Celestial Weather
　　Such enjoyment gives,
We like Birds flock hither,
　　Browzing on green leaves :
Some who late sate Scowling,
　　Publick Cheats to mend ;
Study now with Bowling,
　　Each to Cheat his Friend :
Whilst on the Hawthorn Tree, Terry rerry, rerry, rerry,
　　rerry,
rerry, rerry, sings the Blackbird, Oh what a World
　　have we.

In

In the Eastern Regions,
    Cannibals abound ;
Eas'd of all Religions,
    Man does Man confound :
But our worser Natives,
    Here Church-Rules obey ;
Yet like Barb'rous Caitiffs,
    Gorge up more than they :
In the Town, hot Follies,
    Fools to Faction draw ;
Nonsence, Noise and Malice,
    Passes too for Law :
Whilst in the, &c.

The old Game's again on Trial,
    As our Church-men guess ;
Some write We most Loyal,
    Yet mean nothing less :
Ev'ry Factious Teazer,
    Proudly Votes his Will ;
Praise be then to *Cæsar,*
    Who sits Patient still :
Chanc'ry wants a Ruler,
    Justice Scales to guide ;
S——*ts* want a cooler,
    Who like *Jehu* Ride :
Whilst on the, &c.

Give me then a Bottle,
    Musidora by ;
Wine that warms the Noddle,
    Does all Cares defy :
Sol has enter'd *Aries,*
    Summer Sweets do fall,
Pleasures new and various,
    Let's enjoy 'em all ;

So adieu, State Janglers,
  Our whole Winters Curse ;
Farewel to Law wranglers,
  That so plague the Purse :
Hark in the, &c.

The New BLACKBIRD :

A Song, *in the Wonders of the Sun, or, the
Kingdom of Birds : To the foregoing
Tune.*

WHilst Content is wanting
      In the World below ;
We in freedom chanting,
  Life's true pleasure know :
Cloy'd with care and duty,
  To Superiour sway ;
They ne'er see the Beauty,
  Of one happy Day :
Profits Golden Follies,
  Half the Globe infest ;
Faction, Pride, and Malice,
  Governs all the rest :
*Whilst in eternal Day ; Terry, rerry, rerry, rerry,
Hey, Terry rerry, Sings the* Blackbird,
  Ah ! what a World have they ?

Giant Limb'd Ambition,
  Like a *Tyrant* Reigns ;
Forming new Division
  Hourly in their Brains :
Sometimes Peace enjoying,
  Some they a League begin ;

But

But one *Monarch's* dying,
  Breaks 'em all again ;
Then the grave State-menders,
  For Religion Fight ;
Tho' the hot Pretenders,
  Never had a doit :
Whilst here in lasting Day; Terry, &c.

Warriors all are Princes,
  When their Aid they want ;
Armies for defences,
  Present Pay they grant :
But the work once ended,
  They the Chiefs disown ;
Who in hast disbanded,
  Loudly are cry'd down :
Thus uncur'd they Nourish,
  Whimseys worse Disease ;
Whether lose or Flourish,
  Never are at ease :
Whilst here in lasting Day; Terry, &c.

The fat Pamper'd City,
  Grumbling at the Tax ;
Think to stint, 'tis pitty,
  Bellies or their Backs :
The Rich Country Booby,
  Brooding o'er his Ground ;
Low'rs and wondrous Moody,
  Grudges four in the Pound :
Gospel Fermentation, banters all our Souls ;
  And to Fire the Nation,
Blackcoats blow the Coals :
  Whilst here in lasting Day,
Terry, terry, terry rerry, Sings the Blackbird ;
  Oh ! What a World have they.

The CAMBRIAN *Glory.*

An ODE : *Or ; Memoirs of the Lives and Valiant Actions, of the Ancient* Britains ; *to be Sung every St.* David's *Day.*

BRUTE * who descended from *Trojan* stem,
   First Ancient *Albion* alarm'd with his Forces;
From whom their Ancestors raise their Name,
   Of whose brave Deeds are so many discourses:
And when *Rome's* Eagles aloft did soar,
   Valiant † *Caractacus* with Conduct glorious;
Fought 'em till Fate envying *Britain* power,
   Gave up her Hero a Prize to ‖ *Ostorius*.

CHORUS.

England take Caution,
   By this fam'd Nation;
All agree, whilst your are free,
   And Rich and able:
Friendly treat, you'll be great,
   Quarrel on, you're undone,
Think on the bundle of Rods in the Fable.

Fatal Division first chang'd their Case,
   Jealousie needless, and Fears beyond measure;
Had they combin'd, *Rome* had conquer'd less,
   Nor had § *Casibelan* sold them to *Cæsar:*
But since that Change they can ne'er retrieve,
   Leave we it here for Example in Story;
And now to Honour those since did Live,
   Charm the sweet Lyre with the *Cambrian* Glory.
England *take Caution,* &c.

Of *Wales* and her noble Sons I Sing,
   To whom my Muse has his Trophy erected;
Who, when the first mighty (*a*) Conquering King,
   All others quell'd, yet remain'd unsubjected:
Freedom and Right they all held so dear,
   Rather than yield up the Glory of either;

---

* Brute *Invaded* Britain *Anno Mun.* 2855. † *King of*
Britain. ‖ *Lieutenant in* Britain *for* Claudius *Imp.* § *Sir*
Wm. Temples *Introduct. to Hist. of* England. (*a*) *vid.*
Stows *Annals* of Wm. *the Conqueror.* Anno 1074.

Handfuls of Men against Crowds appear,
   Stoutly resolving to Dye all together.
England *take Caution*, &c.

Rufus the next o'th' Conquering Line,
   Spoyl'd a great Monarch by being a Miser;
He heavy Taxes * the *Welch* assign'd,
   Which, than to Pay him, 'tis known they were wiser:
Bravely they fought, tho' at last home fled,
   Yet had the Victors no wonder to brag on;
For still on the Mountains an Egg was laid,
   That some Years after grew up to a Dragon.
England *take Caution*, &c.

† *Stephen* and ‖ *Henry* the first of the Name,
   Did in each Reign prove the *Griffiths Welch* mettle,
And brave *Cadwallader* lost no fame,
   Tho' by base Treachery slain before Battle:
Valiant K. *John* § too by force of Arms,
   Threatn'd bold *Conan* to lessen his Bravery;
Yet thought fit after to come to terms,
   Welchmen were never yet huff'd into slavery.
England *take Caution*, &c.

But what no force then could do on Earth,
   Policy in the next Reign well affected;
For at *Carnarvan*, (*a*) a Prince had Birth,
   To whom as Country-men they all subjected:
(*b*) Am'rous *Lewellen* too Charm'd with Love,
   Chang'd his Renown for a Wedded condition;
Beauty's soft Joy did so powerful prove,
   That paying Tribute, he veil'd his Ambition.
England *take Caution*, &c.

---

* *Vid.* Stow 7 *year of* K. Wm. Rufus, *Anno* 1094.
† Anno. R. Steph. 1*st.* 1136. ‖ Hen. 2. *Anno.* R. 26.
Anno Dom. 1180. § K. John. *Anno.* 1212. (*a*) *vid.*
Stow. *Anno* R. Ed. 1*st.* 12. *Anno Dom.* 1284. (*b*) *vid.*
Baker R. K. Ed. 1*st.*

Fierce

Fierce *Owen Glendower* * did Annals fill,
   When the fourth *Henry* the Hot-spur Infested;
And in three Battles such numbers did kill,
   He like a Fury was fear'd and detested:
Nor was bold *Teuther* † behind in Fame,
   When Glory call'd him, or Freedom excited;
Who for espousing the Royal Dame,
   Soaring too high had his Lustre benighted.
England *take Caution,* &c.

Undaunted *Vaughn* is ne'er forgot,
   Meridith Jenken, nor *Morgan ap Reuther;*
All Slain at *Edgcott* ‖ that fatal sport,
   Whilst others follow'd the Fortune of *Teuther:*
With many more of Renown'd account,
   Who prov'd that Day by their Valiant endeavour;
None, *British* Valour could e'er surmount,
   None ne'er in Battle behav'd themselves braver.
England *take Caution,* &c.

And now at last I must boldly sing,
   Of the fam'd Leek so renown'd in old story;
First wore in Fight § as a famous thing,
   Wales to distinguish in Conquering Glory:
Coxcombs may Laugh at they know not what,
   Whilst to the Wise I affirm this Relation;
Roses (a) for Trifles great fame have got,
   Onyons (b) been Deified on less occasion.
England *take Caution,* &c.

---

* *Vid.* Stow. *Anno* R. Hen. *4th. Anno Dom.* 1492.
† *vid.* Baker. Hen. *6th. Beheaded for Marrying the
King's Mother.* ‖ *Battle at* Edgcott 9. Ed. *4th. Anno.*
1469. § *Leeks first worn in Honour of a great Victory
won by the* Welch. *When each by wearing one in his
Hat, was distinguish'd from their foes.* (a) *Badges of
the Jarrs 'twixt* York, *and* Lancaster. (b) Onyons
ador'd by Egyptians *as Gods.*

 Merlin

Merlin * the Fam'd who her Native was,
  Prophecy'd still the true worth of this Nation ;
Equal to all if they not surpass,
  For Honour, Courage, and Arts in each station :
Had their cross Stars made 'em e'er unite,
  And against Foes jointly done their endeavour ;
England's proud Name had ne'er seen the Light,
  But *Britain* held up her Title for ever.
    Therefore take Caution,
      By this brave Nation ;
    All agree, whilst you are free,
      And Rich and able :
    Friendly treat, you'll be great,
      Quarrel on, you're undone,
    Think on the Bundle of Rods in the Fable.

---

* Merlin *the Miracle of his Time born in* Britain.

A Song.

I Follow'd Fame and got Renown,
  I rang'd all o'er the Park and Town ;
I haunted Plays, and there grew Wise,
Observing my own modish Vice :
Friends and Wine I next did try,
Yet I found no solid Joy ;
Greatest Pleasures seem too small,
Till *Sylvia* made amends for all.

But see the state of humane Bliss,
How vain our best Contentment is ;
As of my Joy she was the Chief,
So was she too my greatest Grief :
Fate, that I might be undone,
Dooms this Angel but for one ;
And, alass, too plain I see,
That I am not the happy he.

Against

Against Free-Will:

A SONG.

GO silly Mortall, and ask thy Creator,
  Why thy short Life is Tormented with Care ;
Why thou art Slave to the Follies of Nature,
  Why for thy Plague he made Woman so fair ?
      If *Chloes* Glances
      Can charm thy Sences,
  And Beauty force thee into her snare ;
What's this *Free-Will*, of which Gownmen so prate,
When none, none have power to controul their Fate.

If Man be Monarch of all the Creation,
  Women in Reason should stoop to his sway ;
Fair, Rich, or Witty, by free Inclination
  Owning his Priviledge, calmly obey ;
      Else every Brute is
      More blest with Beauties,
  The Horse or Stag, each can seize his Prey ;
Who e'er i'th' Grove saw the Lordly Bull,
Sigh to the fair, She like a loving Fool.

A

A Song *in the* Opera *call'd, The* Kingdom *of the* Birds. *Sung by Miss* Willis.

IN the Fields in Frost and Snows,
  Watching late and early ;
There I keep my Father's Cows,
  There I Milk 'em Yearly :
Booing here, Booing there,
Here a Boo, there a Boo, every where a Boo,
We defy all Care and Strife,
In a Charming Country-Life.

Then

Then at home amongst the Fowls,
   Watching late and early ;
There I tend my Fathers Owls,
   There I feed 'em Yearly :
Whooing here, Whooing there,
Here a whoo, there a whoo, every where a whoo,
We defy all Care and Strife,
In a Charming Country Life.

When the Summer Fleeces heap,
   Watching late and early ;
Then I Shear my Father's Sheep,
   Then I keep 'em Yearly :
Baeing here, Baeing there,
Here a Bae, there a Bae, every where a Bae,
We defy all Care, &c.

In the Morning e'er 'twas light,
   In the Morning early ;
There I met with my Delight,
   Once he Lov'd me dearly :
Wooeing here, Wooeing there,
Here a wooe, there a wooe, every where a wooe,
Oh ! How free from Care, &c.

E'er the Light came from above,
   In the Morning early ;
There I met with my true Love,
   There I met him early :
Wooeing here, Wooeing there,
Here he wooe, there he wooe, every where he wooe,
Oh ! How free from Care, &c.

In the Morn at six of the Clock,
   In the Morning early ;
There I fed our Turkey-Cock,
   There I fed him yearly, cou, cou, goble, goble, goble !
Couing here, Couing there,
Here a cou, there a cou, every where a cou,
Oh ! How free from Care and Strife,
Is a Pleasant Country-Life.

In

In the Morning near the Fens,
  In the Morning early ;
There I feed my Father's Hens,
  There I feed them Yearly :
Cackle here, Cackle there,
Here a cack, there a cack, every where a cack,
Oh ! How free from Care and Strife,
Is a Pleasant Country Life.

In the Morning with good speed,
  In the Morning early ;
I my Father's Ducks do feed,
  In the Morning early :
Quacking here, Quacking there,
Here a quack, there a quack, every where a quack,
Oh ! How free from Care, &c.

In the Morning fair and fine,
  In the Morning early ;
There I feed my Father's Swine,
  There I feed them Yearly :
Grunting here, Grunting there,
Here a grunt, there a grunt, every where a grunt,
Oh ! How free from Care and Strife,
Is a Pleasant Country Life.

To CHLORIS :

An ODE *set to the New Riggadoon.*

I Love thee well,
　But not so well to wed thee,
Lest Blood rebel,
And Appetite should cloy :
　Whilst free and kind,
Each Hour I long to bed thee :
　But if confin'd,
Should scarce believ't a Joy.

[*Second Movement.*]

In Earth and Air
All Creatures else possess
　Their pleasing Liberty ;
Then why should Man,
　The Lord of all the Universe,
Less happy be.

[*Third Movement.*]

Bring Musick then, and Wine still,
　And every one his Dear,
That Friendship most divine still,
　That treats with *Cher éntiér.*

[*Fourth Movement.*]

The Wise think all those very dull,
　To Marriage Yokes incline ;
But if e'er I do play the Fool,
　Dear *Chloris* I am thine.

A

A SONG *made upon a New Country Dance* *at* Richmond, *call'd,* Mr. Lane's Maggot.

STrike up drowsie Gut-scrapers;
  Gallants be ready,
  Each with his Lady;
  Foot it about,
  'Till the Night be run out,
Let no ones humour pall :
Brisk Lads now cut your Capers ;
  Put your Legs to't,
  And shew you can do't,
  Frisk, frisk it away
  'Till break of Day,
And hey for *Richmond* Ball !
  Fortune-Biters,
  Hags, Bum-fighters,
  Nymphs of the Woods,
  And stale City Goods ;

Ye

Ye Cherubins,
And Seraphins,
Ye Caravans,
And Haradans,
In Order all advance :
Twittenham Loobies,
Thistleworth Boobies,
Wits of the Town,
And Beaus that have none ;
Ye Jacobites as sharp as Pins,
Ye Mounsieurs, and ye Sooterkins,
I'll teach you all the Dance.

The DANCE.

Cast off *Tom* behind *Johnny*,
Do the same *Nanny*,
Eyes are upon ye ;
Trip it between
Little *Dickey* and *Jean*,
And set in the Second Row :
Then, cast back you must too,
And up the first Row ;
Nimbly thrust thro' ;
Then, then turn about,
To the left, or you're out,
And meet with your Love below.
Pass, then cross,
Then *Jack's* pretty Lass,
Then turn her about, about and about ;
And *Jack*, if you can do so too,
With *Betty*, whilst the time is true,
We'll all your Ear commend :
Still there's more
To lead all four ;
Two by *Nancy* stand,
And give her your Hand,
Then cast her quickly down below,
And meet her in the second Row :
The Dance is at an end.

The

The Three Goddesses: Or, The Glory of Tunbridge Wells. Made to a Tune of Mr. Barret's.

L Eave, leave the drawing Room,
    Where Flowers of Beauty us'd to bloom,
The Nymph fated to o'ercome,
    Now triumphs at the Wells ;
Shape, Air, and charming Eyes,
Her Face the gay, the grave, and wise,
The Beaus spite of Box and Dice,
    Acknowledge all excels ;
Cease, cease to ask her Name,
The crown'd Muses noblest Theam,
Whose Graces by immortal Fame,
    Should only sounded be :
But if you long to know,
Look round yonder dazling Row,
And who does most like an Angel show,
    You may be sure is she.

See near the Sacred Springs,
That cure to fell Diseases brings,
As loud Fame of Idea sings,
    Three Goddesses appear,
Wealth, Glory too possest,
The third with charming Beauty blest,
So rare Heav'n and Earth confest,
    She conquer'd every where :
Like her this Charmer now,
Makes all Love-sick Gazers bow,
Nay, even Old Age the Flame allow,
    That influences all,
Wealth can no Trophy rear,
Nor bright Fame the Garland wear,
To beauty every *Paris* here,
    Devotes the Golden Ball.

A

*A Health to the Imperialists; Or, An In-
vective* ODE *on the Treachery of the
Elector of* Bavaria.   *To a Tune of
Mr.* J. C.

ULM is gone,
But basely won,
And treacherous *Bavaria* there has buried his Renown ;
That stroling Prince,
Who few Years since,
Was cramm'd with *William's* Gold :
Pension lost,
And hopes too crost,
Of having more
From *Brittish* store,
To keep his wonted post ;
To aid in vain,
Usurping *Spain,*
Himself to *France* has sold :
For 'tis plain,
Tho' Plots were vain,
That *Ausburgh* was th' intended Project of his Brain ;
The

The Mem'ry of *Nassaw*,
Was valu'd not a Straw,
Had *Mounsieur* reliev'd *Landau*;
Let him go,
A worthless Foe,
And whilst the Princes round resolve his overthrow;
A jolly Bottle bring,
Great *Baden's* Praises sing,
And th' *Roman's* valiant King.

Lost in Fame,
Involv'd in Shame,
Thou odious Scandal to the noble *Maximilian's* name,
Who durst debase,
Imperial Grace,
And thus provoke the *Ban*,
Honour slight,
And Royal Right,
Expected daily by the Circles on their sides to fight;
For *Spain's* ill Cause,
And *French* Kickshaws,
Turn basely cat in Pan;
But go on,
Forlorn undone,
And e'er his yearly Course around has rowl'd the Sun;
Deserted and disgrac'd,
Still routed too and chac'd,
In Chains thou may'st grown thy last:
Or may Fate,
To prove her Hate,
Thy Falshood to the Misery of War translate;
And there so low appear,
A Fuzee may'st thou bear,
Like some poor Musqueteer.

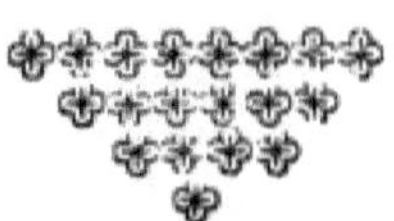

Prince

Prince Eugene's *Health.* A Song *set by Mr.* John Barret.

YOU the glorious Sons of Honour,
    That each Hour your Fame advance;
Pray take notice in what manner,
   Lewis prizes it in *France:*
In the *Reswick* Charte remember,
  He great *William* lawful names;
But grown doating last *September*,
  Loudly sounds, loudly sounds up another *James:*
Routs our Trade too,
And wou'd no doubt invade too;
Could he turn the *Oglio*
Into *Seine*, which our Boys in *Italy*,
All resolve shall never be,
Drink, drink, drink, drink we then a flowing Glass
    to Prince *Eugene.*

Like

Like the Peasant in the Fable,
   As we read in times of old,
Rated from the Satyrs Table,
   For his blowing hot and cold
From his own, and every Nation,
   Mounsieur should be rated so :
Who on every vile Occasion,
   With all sorts of Winds can blow :
Sign a Peace too,
And break it with as much Ease too,
   Take an Oath now, and strait deny't again ;
But that this and all that's past,
May come home to him at last,
   Prosper may the conquering Arms of Prince *Eugene.*

With despotick Resolution,
   He from Subjects Gold can tear ;
Praise be to our Constitution,
   We have no such doings here :
Government in blest Condition,
   When to just Law 'tis confin'd ;
But tyrannick Disposition,
   Ne'er yet agreed with the *English* kind ;
Whilst *Carero*,
Combin'd with Gallick *Nero ;*
Anjou's Crown then unjustly would maintain,
   And th'Imperial Claim controul ;
Cheering still each Heart and Soul,
   Let us see the Glass go round to Prince *Eugene.*

                                             The

The Scotch VIRAGO.

A SONG *Sung to the Queen at* Kensington.
The Words made to a pretty New Scotch
Tune.

VAliant *Jockey's* march'd away,
    To fight the Foe with brave *Mackay;*
Leaving me, poor Soul, forlorn,
To Curse the Hour when I was Born;
But, I've sworn Ise follow too;
And dearest *Jockey's* Fate pursue;
Near him be to Guard his precious Life,
Never *Scot* had such a Loyal Wife:
     Sword Ise wear,
     Ise cut my Hair,
Tann my Cheeks, that once were thought so fair;
     In Souldier's Weed,
     To him I'll speed,
Never sike a Trooper cross'd the *Tweed.*

Trumpet sound to Victory,
Ise kill (my self) the next *Dundee;*
Love, and Fate, and Rage, do all agree,
To do some glorious Deed by me:
Great *Bellona*, take my part,
Fame and Glory, charm my Heart;
That for Love, and bonny *Scotland's* good,
Some brave Action may deserve my Blood:
     Nought shall appear,
     Of Female fear,
Fighting by his Side, I Love so dear;
     All the *North* shall own,
     There ne'er was known
Such a sprightly Lass, this thousand Years.

On

On the Queen's Progress to the BATH.

Dear *Jack* if you mean
      To be cur'd of the Spleen,
Or know any Neighbour that has it ;
      Tho' ill Humours sway
      From a *Hypocondra*,
You may do it by reading the *Gazette.*

      The Q——n you know late,
      Made a Progress in state,
From whence may come wonderful matter :
      And furnish fine Tales,
      When a New P—— of *Wales*,
Proceeds from the happy *Bath-waters.*

      But this is not it,
      That the flatus will fit,
Or make the dull Reader grow merry :
      Nor to tell the Renown
      Of Old *Oxford's* fine Town,
And how they did chant it down derry.

      For should I bring in
      The grave Vice, or the Dean,
Or at School-boys Verses should nibble ,
      Or the Presents that serv'd,
      So pat I deserv'd,
To have my Head broke with the Bible.

      Nor Mirth can we raise
      Upon *Badminton* place,
Nor rally his Grace's good Table :
      Nor on *Gloucestershire* Knights,
      Who the News-monger writes,
Were preferr'd by the Right Honourable.

      Nor make we Remarks
      On the bluff Country Sparks,
Who gallop'd, no Fury cou'd stop 'em :
      All ty'd to their Swords,
      Like so many Lords,
Being led up by *Blathwait* and *Popham.*

But

But it's here you will laugh,
For a Mile and a half,
Coming near to *Bath's* flourishing City ;
There appear'd such a Rout
From the Sheds round about,
Gave occasion to furnish my Ditty.

Some 200 young Jades,
Jolly bouncing Cook-maids,
Came romping to taste the Q——s Bounty ;
All Virgins we hear,
From the false *Gazetteer*,
When by G—— there's scarce five in the County.

But such as they were
They in Order appear,
Tho' no *Cynthia* there, nor *Astrea;*
For with Arrows and Bows,
Each look'd like a Blouze,
Instead of a *Penthesilea.*

The Kitchins in Town
Were all left alone,
And on the Stairs Cobwebbs were hanging ;
When *Sue, Kate,* and *Doll*
Were imping *Whitehall*,
Before an old Crowd that stood twanging.

Then plump bobbing *Joan*,
Strait call'd for her own,
And thought she frisk'd better than any ;
'Till *Sisly* with Pride,
Took the Fiddler aside,
And bid him strike up Northern *Nanny*.

Who in Country Fairs
Had e'er seen the Bears,
Hop round when the Keeper does strike 'em ?
For Airs, and for Steps,
For Faces and Shapes,
These Virgins would fancy just like 'em.

Thus

Thus hot with Renown,
They come dancing to Town,
All full of their highly deserving ;
    Each freckl'd Face Jade,
    Upon Royalty fed,
Whilst the Lodgers at home were a starving.

    The Piggs were scarce turn'd,
    And the Turkeys half burn'd,
To add to the Fame of the Nation ;
    The Mutton half boyl'd,
    And the Pullets all spoil'd,
For the Turnspits were all in Procession.

    But here comes the Cross,
    For the Jackets that cost
Forty Pounds, for loyally shewing,
    As some Authors say,
    The good Queen is to pay,
Or must to the City be owing.

    Which Scandal profound
    Made 'em stir their Strumps round,
Whilst each Lass her Courtier engages ;
    For should they be slow,
    And Sir *Ben.* should say no,
The poor Jades must do't out of their wages.

    Who glowing with Heat,
    So rosie, so neat,
Each look'd as to Marriage she'd chose one :
    And some that can tell,
    Say they danc'd too as well,
As the famous *Subligny,* or *Dowson.*

A

A New ODE

On the Bel Assembly *in* Kensington *Garden, one Summer Evening, when the Princess was there.*

NOW the Summer solstice does scorching come,
      Dust gives Air no room,
      Roses scarce can bloom,
Of all famous Gardens by Nature blest,
Beauty has confest *Kensington* the best :
Bright *Belviaera*, with gracious Airs,
With the Angels, who born from her,
      The sweetest of all Fairs,
      Thither oft repairs ;
Then thro' the Walks, if you cast your Eyes,
You will think the bright Stars descended with all
    rapting Joys,
      Did your Soul surprise,
      Did your Soul surprise.

When the glorious *Phœbus* declining shews
      See the splendid Rows,
      Gawdy Nymphs and Beaus,
See the beauteous Labrynth where Lovers meet,
      And with Voices sweet,
      Amorous Songs repeat,
Vows to each Mistress, Gallants pursue,
And the Nymphs there to answer them
      Shew Passion, but not true,
      As their Lovers do.
Thus the World's Genius Intreague invades,
And Mankind, when Love makes 'em fond,
      Court in these pleasant Shades,
      Widows, Wives, and Maids.

The

The Comical Dreamer.

LAST Night a Dream came into my Head,
Thou wert a fine white Loaf of Bread ;
Then if *May* Butter I cou'd be,
How I wou'd spread,
Oh ! how I wou'd spread my self on thee :

This

This Morning too my Thoughts ran hard,
That you were made a cool Tankard ;
Then cou'd I but a Lemon be,
     How I wou'd squeese,
Oh ! how I wou'd squeese my Juice in thee.

Lately when Fancy too did roam,
Thou wert my dear, a Honey-comb ;
And had I been a pretty Bee,
     How I wou'd suck,
Oh ! how I wou'd creep, creep into thee :
A Vision too I had of old,
That thou a Mortar wert of Gold ;
Then cou'd I but the Pestle be,
     How I wou'd pound,
Oh ! how I wou'd pound my Spice in thee.

Once too my Dream did Humour take,
Thou wert a Bowl of *Hefford's* Rack ;
Z ——— cou'd I then the Ladle be,
     How wou'd I pour,
Oh ! how wou'd I pour out Joys from thee.
Another time by Charm divine,
I dreamt thou wert an Orchard fine ;
Then cou'd I but thy Farmer be,
     How I wou'd plant,
Oh ! how I wou'd plant my Fruit in thee.

Soon after Whims came in my Pate,
Thou wert a Pot of Chocolate ;
And cou'd I but the Rowler be,
     How wou'd I rub,
Oh ! how wou'd I twirl, and froth up thee :
But since all Dreams are vain my Dear,
Let now some solid Joy appear ;
My Soul still thine is prov'd to be, let body now,
     Let Body now with Soul agree.

A

A SONG *in the fourth Act of the* Modern Prophets.

ELevate your joys, ye inspir'd of the Town,
    The *Camizars* are come, are come ;
To Instruct and confute the black Gown,
    Germany and *France* have been dancing the Jigg :
And now they fain, they fain, they fain,
    Would new model the *Tory* and *Whigg;*
They Preach and they Pray, the Spirit moves,
And then they shake, and quake, and *Gambols* they
        play,
            This Divine they call,
And gathers up the Mob, the Devil and all.

Pillorys we laugh at, and Infamy there,
    The loss of Ears, and Lash
We Frantickly think is an Honour to bear ;
    Round about the Nation thus Madly we go,
And where we find the Fools
    Are most Fertile, our Tenets we sow :
            A change we'd obtain,
Which to effect we hum and ha, and Proselytes gain :
            Eagerly they come,
And Joyn to promote Rebellion at home.

Salley's

Salley's *Answer to* Sawney : *A New* SONG.

AS I gang'd o'er the Links of *Leith*
    One Morn, was fresh and rosie;
The Birds did sing, the Flowers did breath
    So sweet, I sought a Poesie :
I thought I heard one Sing my praise,
    And found 'twas sweet and bonny;
And sounded *Sally* with such grace,
    It must be Charming *Sawney.*

His Daddy, was a Farmer grey,
    That lov'd the Barn and Mow, Sir;
Brisk *Sawney* train'd another way,
    Can Pipe, as well as Plough, Sir :
He'd touch a Flute, and play a Tune
    So soft, so sweet and bonny;
Each *Philomel* that heard fell down,
    And died to Eccho *Sawney.*

I often went to Milk our Kine,
    Inspir'd with Love and Folly :
And there he'd Chant a song Divine,
    And close with Lovely *Sally :*
The Teats I stroak'd, whence Milk did flow,
    His words too drop'd down Honey;
And ev'ry Note did charm me so,
    I ran half Mad for *Sawney.*

He press'd my Hand and hugg'd my Wast,
    A Kiss did then avail too;
And often he my Labour eas'd,
    With carrying home my Pail too :
He ask'd my Dad, for me to Wife,
    Who said, to have more Money;
A Neighbouring Loon should ease that strife,
    But I resolv'd for *Sawney.*

Then

Then soon my Mother took my part,
  This Girl we must not baulk so ;
There's something sad, grows near her Heart,
  Her Face is Pale as Chalk too :
And now 'tis done, the Steeple rings,
  We each call Joy and Honey ;
Whilst I despise the Crowns of Kings,
  I'm pleas'd so well with *Sawney*.

To CHLORIS.

A SONG.

C Hloris, for fear you should think to deceive me,
  Know all my Life I have studied your kind ;
Learn'd in your *Grammar*, I'd have you believe me,
  And all your Tricks in my Practice you'll find :
    Ogling and Glances,
    Sighs and advances,
Poor Country Cully no more shall ensnare ;
    Pantings and Tremblings,
    Fits and Dissemblings,
Now you must leave, and Intrigue on the Square.

Give me the Girl that's good natur'd and Witty,
  Whose pleasant Talk can her Friend entertain ;
One who's not Proud, if you tell her she's Pretty,
  And yet enough to be Honest and Clean :
    Pox on Town Cheatings,
    Jilts and Cognettings,
I my Dear *Chloris*, will bring up by Hand,
    Tears and Complainings,
    Breed but Disdainings,
Those still Love best that are under Command.

A SATYR *Sung in Parts : Being the Widow Tickle-*Toby's *Model to the* Common Councel, *and* Livery-men *of* London. *Humbly recommending to their Choice : And giving a true and Ingenious Character of Four Worthy Candidates for the next ensuing Parliament,* Viz. *Sir* Tho. Ab—y, *Sir* Rob. Cl—n, *Sir* Wm. A—t, *and* G. He— *Esq.*

C H O R U S.

These, these are fit Members my Brethren, don't lose 'em,
But if you'd be sure of good Patriots, Chuse 'em.

Right Thrifty, and wisely Honest Brethren,

FULL Forty long Years as a Freeholder's Wife,
   I led in the City a Conjugal Life ;
As Honest as Wise, you may take't on my Word,
And Smock still up lifted, in fear of the Lord :
We our *Consciences* settled too, at the first Greeting,
So he went to Chappel, and I to the *Meeting ;*
Thus Cunningly saving our Bacon both ways,
We still made the Best of late Troublesom Days :
And as a right Conjugal Tempter oft learns,
By loud Curtain Lectures, or Pillow Concerns,
Her Husband's best Secrets, so I for a Kiss,
Whenc'er I thought fitting to Pump him, knew his :
No matter pass'd in *Common-Councel*, of weight,
So private in th' Morn, but I knew it at Night ;
At the Pricking of Sheriffs, I could tell who would Sign,
To the chargeable Office, or else pay the Fine :
Of chusing Lord Mayors too, I found the Intrigue,
And knew which would carry't, the *Tory* or *Whigg ;*
What Tricks on the Hustings *Fanaticks* would play,
And how the *Church* Party were still kept at Bay :
With Bribery Cheats and perverting the Law,
From the First of King *JAMES* to the 12*th* of *Nassau.*

N ow

Now having some Reason to think I am Wise,
I hope my good Brethren you'll take my Advice;
Who still fancy'd Business e're Years I knew Ten,
And have ever since been a Dealer with Men:
Know Court Spies as well as the Fathers that got 'em,
And who 'mongst the Crowd will prove good at the
    bottom;
In Naming Four Patriots worth the perusing,
This Juncture whilst now you are Candidates chusing:
Whose Worth the most Famous of Poets should Sing,
Whose Vertue, Wit, Learning, and Zeal for the King;
Were never outvy'd since Furr'd Gowns sat in Chairs,
At the End of large Halls, or *London* had Mayors:
Or since Eighty Three with a Plot at the End on't
Or th' first bold *Church Prætor*, to the last Independant.

The Character of Sir Rob. Cl—n.

The First I present, is a Reverend Knight,
Who tho' of small reading 'tis well known can Write
Noverint Universi, done in a fair Hand,
Having chows'd many Fops both of Money and Land:
Obliging himself still as well as the Nation,
By Art of Procuring, and Continuation;
With *Conscience* strait-laced the Grave Justice of Peace,
Has oft let out Money the Needy to ease:
But never was known, search the City quite round,
For Interest to take above Ten in the Pound;
Or if the poor Unthrift in Payment was dodging,
Refus'd to provide him the Counter for Lodging:
By which, and by what for Forbearance was given,
He grew mighty Rich in the Service of Heaven;
Tho' as to his Church some will tell you this Tale,
He's right Linsey Wolsey, half Mild and half Stale:
So Mixt he shall go with Sir *Charles* to St. *Paul*,
Next Day with Sir *Humphry* to *Pin-makers Hall;*
'Tis true in the Days of King *CHARLES* 'twas all clear,
When this worthy Magistrate sate in the Chair:
When Baits for the Treasury Banquets were made,
And Beautiful Dame was in Scarlet Array'd;

         Then

Then High *Tory* Interest shone plainly at Home,
No properer Emblem was nearer than *Rome :*
But now the neglect of known Merit which sways ⎫
The Hearts of the Zealous, these *Sanctified* Days, ⎬
He turns Cat in Pan, and new Glory to raise ;   ⎭
Tho' both in his Sense, and his Loyalty limber,
Resolves to do Mischief, and stand for a Member.

Chorus of Stationers, Tally-men, Pawn-brokers,
      Bayliffs, and their Wives and Families.

These, these are the Members my Brethren, don't lose 'em,
But if you'd be sure of good Patriots, Chuse 'em.

Character of Sir Wm. Ash—t.

The next, is one, late took the Prætors grand Oath,
O'th' top of Professions too, dealing in Cloth ;
Looks great as a Baron in *Westminster* Dome,
As proudly too sits on the Wool-packs at Home :
Austere in his Method, Phantastick in Gate,
Conceited of Parts, like that Maggot *Will. P—*
And with a Thumb'd *Horace* still shewn from his Pocket,
Makes all the Wise laugh at the *Classical* Blockhead :
Who tho' he has umbrage of Shop and a Trade,
Detraction, and Impudence still gets his Bread ;
This Patron of Clothiers late plac'd in the Chair,
Resolv'd to give proof of a Wonderful Mayor :
Beginning with strange Orders to grace his high Station,
And plant in the City severe Reformation ;
And tho' Law and Justice were of slender growth,
Within his Quag Brain being ignorant of both :
He soon got a Clark, by whose Faculties strong,
All matters were done, which confirms the old Song ;
That Honour's but Air, and proud Flesh but Dust is,
'Tis the Commons make Laws, as th' Clark makes the
      Justice :
Bluff Constables were his best Favourites still,
Who daily and hourly brought Grist to the Mill ;
My Lord I affirm, this Man Thirteen Oaths swore,
That's Thirteen good Shillings you know to the Poor :
                                        That

That *TORY* was Drunk, and (oh Monstrous !) pray
      note,
Here's one, tho' 'tis Sunday prophaning a Boat ;
At which the grave Magistrate twirling his Chain,
Delinquent too standing by fretting with Pain ;
Crys out to his Clark, with a Voice full of Awe,
Here turn to the Statute, and shew him the Law :
To sit in the Stocks, or pay Fine of a Crown,   )
He also for the Twelve-pence more must lay down,   }
Thus Sentence is past, and away Struts the Gown.   )
Whilst the Money that this way was stripp'd from the
      Donor,
Went part to th' Informer, the rest to his Honour ;
Thus, thus was the Year of his Dignity past,
By which may be well his Integrity guest :
And if of's Religion, and Wisdom you'll speak,
The one is Wool-gathering, the other to seek ;
Yet fancy's he should be a Chief amongst those,
Who serve their Dear Country with Ays, & with No's.

Chorus of Clothiers, Packers, Taylors, Botchers, their
      Wives, Sisters, and Daughters.

These, these are fit Members my Brethren don't lose 'em,
But if you'd be sure of good Patriots, Chuse 'em.

The Character of Sir Tho. Ab—y, *a Linnen-Draper.*

The next altho' he give out in the Bill,
He's Loyal a *Church-man,* and able at VVill ;
Yet is as most think, who his Inside have scann'd,
A rank Independent, as ever wore *Band :*
And tho' some *Sect* Brewers to new make the Man,
VVould fain boil him down to a Presbyter *John ;*
Yet he holds his own still, nor lessens at all,
From ways of Fore-Fathers, in Days of old Noll :
He lately was Mayor too, Sir *Charles* to bereave,
Tho' never at *Church* till then, since he was Sheriff ;
Nor never intends it whilst *Meetings* look Trim,
Or th' *Sisters* wear Lockram, and buy it of him :
                                        Unless

Unless to be Qualified just in this Minute,
To sell all new Shirts to the Dons of the Senate ;
For his Understanding by Ell and by Yard,
Far more than by Politicks finds a Regard :
And yet he wou'd fain be a Patriot too,
Tho' Voting for Candles is all he could do ;
So vile is the Obstinate Will of the Creature,
In thwarting of Providence, Reason, and Nature :
Who all did concur he should get an Estate,
Vend Smocks to the Fair, and propitiously Cheat ;
But never design'd him to be a Law-mender,
No more than a True *Church* of *England* Defender.

Chorus of Pedlars, Choiresters, Cooks, Butlers, Inn-
keepers, and their Wives and Families.

These, these are fit Members my Brethren, don't lose 'em,
But if you'd be sure of good Patriots, Chuse 'em.

The Character of G. Heath *Esq; one of the New*
E. India *Company, and Bank.*

The last I present, is a Teazer o'th' Nation.
Wove fast in the New *India* Association ;
Twin Brother with *Sh—p—d*, of late so ill fated,
And narrowly 'scap'd too, like him to be baited :
For he was as deep in the Bribing Abuse,
For getting false Patriots into the House :
And cram'd full of Wealth, hop'd to gild o're his Crimes
With Metal that all human Mischief sublimes :
'Tis said having store of that cause of all Ills,
Not gain'd by Uprightness, but *Exchequer* Bills ;
When poor Paper Credit, was forc'd on poor Men,
Who Trading for Twenty, were glad to take Ten :
Then, then was his Harvest to Reap, as to Sow,
And rais'd him to stand for a Candidate now ;
For Money can make what you wish, or can think,
And him a Law-maker, who once bore a Link :
Oh happy the Sages that liv'd in old Times,
E'er Faction and Knavery spread into Crimes ;

No Members were then, but of Candor and Worth,
In Learning Exemplary, honour'd in Birth:
Now the Boys can the Suffrages get of the People,
That only talk Bawdy, and know how to Tipple;
And tho' they both Beardless, and Brainless appear,
Are Dignified oft to be Knights of the Shire:
If Mortals then so Insignificant may,
On greatest Affairs of the Land make Essay;
Appear in the Senate, nay, offer a Speech,
A known Wealthy Citizen sure that is Rich:
And one whose small Faults were but Trifles to teaze ye,
As paying in Paper, what should have been Specie;
Or else with two Thirds, and Discounting the rest,
May sit in the House yet as well as the rest.

Chorus of *India* Traders, Exchequer-Men, Bank-
Officers, Tally-Men, *&c.*

*These, these are fit Members my Brethren, don't lose 'em,
But if you'd be sure of good Patriots, Chuse 'em.*

A SONG: *Occasion'd by a broken String of Mrs.* M—— S—— *Viol.*

THE Instrument with which to Sing
    Romana, oft my Ears did bless;
Neglected now with broken String,
    Deny'd the long'd-for Happiness.

Till I resolv'd to lose no part
    Of Joy, and taught by Love the way;
Devoted one that Strung my Heart,
    Provided she would Sing and Play.

Then Musick sweeter than the Spheres,
    That from her Hands and Lips did fall;
My Soul so Ravish'd through my Ears,
    My Heart ne'er felt its loss at all.

To

To PHILLIS; *upon her Complaint for being Lampoon'd.*

PHillis when your ogling Eye
    Betrays your wanton Vanity,
Rail not if a Stander by,
    Does all your Thoughts explain :
When you prim or screw your Face,
Or flutter in fantastick Dress,
Blame not Wit if Rhimes express,
    The Vice of things so vain :
If you wou'd be fam'd for Sence,
And scrupe Severity of Pen,
Lay by your Pride, and still provide
    For Graces of the Mind :
For let Vertue like the Sun,
Extend its Rays when all is done,
'Tis very rare the Wise and Fair,
    To meet in Woman-kind.

Another

Another SONG *belonging to the last.*

Y ET we Love ye most,
　　When with Satyrs we move ye most ;
All the parts of our Hearts,
Are most fond when we
Seem to reprove ye most ;
'Tis a Vanity that belongs to Humanity,
To think Railing prevailing,
And proper to bring you to Lenity.

Hold your own a while,
And defend but the Town a while,
Now Smile, and then cunningly,
Cunningly, cunningly Frown a while ;
The masculine Creature,
Will be a slave to your Feature still,
And you all wear a Charm to impose,
Upon humane Nature still.

A

A DIALOGUE

Between PHILANDER, *and* SYLVIA.

Philan.

Philan. IN a Desart in *Greenland*,
   Where the Sun ne'er cast an Eye ;
In Contempt of all the World,
   I wou'd live with thee my Joy.
Sylvia. On the Sands of scorcht *India*,
   Where the Sun-burnt Natives fry,
Blest with thee, my dear *Philander*,
   I do chuse to live and dye.
Philan. No nymph with her sly charming Art,
   E'er shall have pow'r to steal my Heart ;
Thou art all in all in every part,
Each Vein of me shall ever be,
Panting with Love of thee.
Sylvia. No Swain with his Wealth, Wit or Art,
   E'er shall have power to storm my Heart.
Thou art all in all in every part,
Each Vein of me will ever be,
Panting with Love of thee.

Philan. Let the Monarch's Ambition,
   Seek new Empire to obtain,
Let the Miser sell his Soul,
   To encrease his slavish Gain.
Sylvia. Let the politick Gown-man,
   Tread the Mazes of the State,
Let the Reverend Divine,
   Teach Mankind decrees of Fate.
Philan. Give me the dear Nymph I adore,
   Happy or Unlucky, Rich or Poor,
Of bounteous Heaven I'd ask no more,
   Nor ever care who's Rich or Fair,
There's all the World in her.
Sylvia. Let no Cloud of Ill Fortune rise,
   To shade me fron *Philander's* Eyes,
Farewel ye World deluding's Joys,
   No charm would seem worth my esteem,
I have all I wish in him.

The *Dissapointed* BEAU.

Made for the Right Honourable and Incom-parable the Lady Emillia Taffe.

STELLA, with Heart controling Grace,
   Young *Hylas* at first sight surpriz'd ;
The Beau that knew his Luckless Face,
   Runs to his Glass to be advis'd :
Tell me, said he, what I shall wear,
How Curl, or how adorn my Hair,
     This Charmer to Command :
What taking Dress shall I put on,
To bring this Tassel gently down,
     And Lure to my Hand.

The God of Love that heard, reply'd,
   Fond Fool, aspire not to possess ;
Her Angel Mind averse to Pride,
   Desert Esteems, and not the Dress :
To thee she will no more Incline,
The mighty *Jove* the Joys Divine,
     That Crown'd his Paradise ;
To him that hopes to be a Saint,
By Powdering, Patching, and by Paint,
     Instead of Sacrifice.

On

On a Beautiful *Young* LADY, *walking in* HAM-WALKS.

W AS it some Cherubin,
   Sent down my Soul to win ;
Or was it Beauties Queen,
   Blessing the Grove :
Was it a Star from high,
   Dropp'd from the Gallery :
Or some Divinity,
   Ranging above.
No, no, no, ah ! no, no, no,
   'Twas Soul delighting *Celemene;*
She whose Grace,
And Charming Face,
   Inspires all with Love.

The

The KING's *Health:*

A CATCH *Sung in Parts.*

NOW Second *Hannibal* is come;
　　O'er frozen Lakes and Mounts of Snow,
To found our Faith on conquer'd *Rome*,
　And give Proud *France* a fatal Blow.

　Well may our *Phœbus* disappear,
And set his Glory in the Sea;
　If Planets of a lower Sphere,
Can give us greater light than he.

　Fryars and Monks, and all those bald-pate Fools,
VVith VVafers, Oyntments, Beads and Shams,
　Pardons, and Antichristian Bulls,
Must yield to *Belgick* battering Rams.

　Infallibility is gone,
And Judges of dispensing Powers,
　That had their Country quite undone,
VVas ever known such Sons of VVhores?

　Drink all around, then by consent,
Health to the Monarch of the Land,
　The Queen, and healing Parliament;
Pledge me Six Bumpers in a Hand.

　And when the Jesuits you see,
Dangling upon the Tripple Tree,
　Fill up Six more, and Sing with me,
A Plague on senseless Popery.

LYRICAL VERSES : *Set to a pleasant Aire, made for the Entertainment, and most humbly Dedicated to the Honourable and Worthy Members of the* OCTOBER CLUB.

THE Thundring *JOVE,*
    In his Radiance above,
Looking down from the lofty Skies ;
    To hear how the Peace,
    Britains comforts increase,
By the Echoes of Sounding Joys :
    All Parties he view'd,
    Both the Bad and the Good,
Like himself then, his Voice did raise ;
    I think fit you should know,
    Of all Clubs here below,
The *October* deserves most praise.

    Apollo stood by,
    Who the hint took with Joy,
And the *Muses* did strait Command ;
    The Members there met,
    Loyal, Honest and Great,
Should be foremost all o'er the Land :
    An Order was made,
    And as soon was obey'd,
Whilst in tuneful Poetick Lays,
    They Harmoniously shew,
    Of all Clubs here below,
The *October* deserves most Praise.

    Let Fame tell the Queen,
    Ever Great and Serene,
When these true *Brittish* Sons appear ;
    Whose Hearts firm have stood,
    For their Country's good,
All that's Loyal and Brave is there :

Succession

　　　　Succession they Joyn,
　　　　To the *HANNOVER* Line,
Yet the Queen wish long Happy Days:
　　　　Thus perpetually shew,
　　　　Of all Clubs here below,
The *October* deserves most Praise.

To the Beauty of New BAGINGTON, *Dear Miss* BROMELY :

A Billet doux *in Return of her* Verses.

YOU Write of Rural Springs
　　And Groves, and name such pretty things,
　　　　That Kings would wish t' Enjoy 'em ;
Besides, you spread such Beauty there,
That could I Pens from Muses share,
　　　　I'm sure I should Employ 'em.

You seem methinks to speak my Praise,
And Write in Verse, but my Young Days,
　　　　Ne'er learnt a Stile so Civil,
Nor could I think you had the power,
But to my head comes Mrs. ——
　　　　And she's in Rhime the Devil.

Yet when I answer you, dear Heart,
It must be Verse in every Part,
　　　　And hear I let you try me ;
Tho' she's a Devil, I shall not care,
My Lines shall Sing y'are Kind, Sweet and Fair,
　　　　For *D'Urfey* now stands by me.

　　　　　　　The

The Second SONG *in the Second* MASQUE.

Set to an Aire, the Character, A Maid of
HONOUR.

A Virgin's Life who would be leaving,
    Free from Care and fond Desire,
Ne'er deceiv'd, or e'er deceiving,
    Loving none, yet all Inspire :
We sit at Home, and Knot the Live-long Day,
A Thousand pretty harmless things we say,
But not one Word of Wedlock's frightful Noose,
For fear we chance to think what we must lose.

Our Souls are free from dire revenges,
    Bosoms Mischief never owns,
Our Wit's Employ'd in making Fringes,
    And Embroidering our Gowns,
If any Lover comes to play the Thief,
Our Natural dear cunning gives relief,
We Sing, we Dance, the tedious Hours away,
And when we've nothing else to do, we pray.

A

A Song *in the Fifth* Masque.

The Character, A Jolly Toping Country Gentleman.

WHen I Visit Proud *Cælia* just come from my
    Glass,
She tells me I'm Fluster'd, and look like an Ass,
When I mean of my Passion to put her in Mind,
She bids me leave Drinking or she'll ne'er be Kind :
That she's charmingly Handsom, I very well know,
And so is my Bottle, each Bumper so too,
And to leave my Soul's Joy, oh ! tis Nonsence to ask,
Let her go to the Devil, to the Devil, bring the tother
    half Flask.

Had she tax'd me with Gaming and bad me forbear,
'Tis a thousand to one I had lent her an Ear,
Had she found out my *Chloris* up three pair of Stairs,
I had baulk't her, and gone to St. *James's* to Prayers,
Had she bid me read Homilies three times a Day,
She perhaps had been humour'd with little to say,
But at Night to deny me my Flask of dear Red,
Let her go to the Devil, to the Devil, there's no more
    to be said.

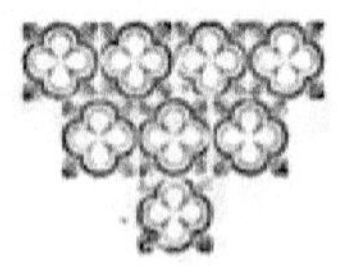

The fond SHEPHERDESS's *Huy-and-*
Cry after her Heart.

A SONG.   *Set to a Pleasant Airc.*

OH yes! Oh yes! Oh yes! I cry,
    Pray tell you gentle Swains hard by,
If you a Roving Heart have met,
Did lately from my Bosom get.

Some Marks to know it I'll Express,
It comes of Loyal Honest Race,
By Nature kind, and prone to Love,
And Constant as the Turtle-Dove.

Upon the outside of the same,
You'll find the Charming *Damon's* Name,
By Love Ingrav'd and plain to show,
From which fresh drops of Gore do flow.

Tis tender as soft down can be,
Or Beauty in its Infancy,
No Wealth can make it e'er untrue,
Such Hearts as mine you'll find but few.

That 'twas Confin'd I late was told,
Amongst the Lambs in *Cupid's* Fold ;
If so, pray seek that Deity,
And carry this Resolve from me.

If he'll restore my Heart again,
I'll keep it from deceits of Men,
From wily Wits and Am'rous Tongues,
And all that to their Sex belongs.

But if this Heart he'll me refuse,
For 'tis a Jewel few would lose ;
Pray let him tell dear *Damon* this,
And in Exchange command me his.

EPI-

EPITALAMY *on the Marriage of the Right Honourable the Lady* Essex Roberts.

RUN Lovers, run before her,
   Kneel once more and adore her,
      The Hour is posting on,
      When all our Joy
      Below the Sky,
      Will be for ever gone.
Tho' Sighs inflame the Air,
And a thousand Eyes are Raining,
No Art nor no Complaining
Can now retreive the Fair ;
She's gone, alass, she's gone,
Then welcome sad Despair.

   See, *Hymen* there attending,
The God of Love descending
      In *Sylvia's* Fetters lies,
      Not all his Art,
      Could guard his Heart
      From her victorious Eyes :
Whose Fair, but cruel Breast,
Refus'd each Shepherd's Passion,
A Torment like Damnation,
To make *Philander* blest,
Whilst he, the happy he,
Of Heaven is sole possest.

   Hail then belov'd *Philander*,
Thou blest, thou glad Commander,
      Of all the World holds rare,
      Innobled Blood,
      The Wise, the Good,
      The Vertuous and the Fair.

               The

The Choice of Heavens store
Is thrown to thy Embraces ;
Such Beauty, Wit, and Graces,
Ne'er deck'd our Plains before,
Nor could Fate study how
To bless a Mortal more.

The HEALTH.

[Second Movement.]

A DIEU to Virginity,
    That silly strange nothing, that Maids are so
        fond of,
Room, Room, for the Bridegroom, he,
All Beauties dear Trophies has now the command of ;
Banish all thoughts of resty *Diana,*
Crown the full Bowl, a Health to *Lucina.*
VVho e'er the Year be run,
Gives the fair Bride a Son,
Able, able, to pledge his own.

A *Comical* DIALOGUE

Between blunt English JOHNNY, *and his Wife* Scotch GIBBY, *about Modern Affairs: Introduced by way of Prologue; in Prose.*

Enter *Gibby*, and *Johnny* after her.

Johnny. **H**Oyday, *why wither away so vast I wonder?*

Gibby. *Gud seth* Johnny *een back to* Edinbrough, *Ise stay no longer amongst your Squablers, Gin I do, I shall Scawld like a Fish-Wife: So Ise gang quietly heam to a Bannock of Barly.*

Johnny. *You shant go* Gibby.

Gibby. *Introth* Johnny *but I will.*

Johnny. *You shant ye Fool, I'll Sing ye out of your Humour.*

Gibby. *Weel, weel, I can Sing too, but for aw that, Ise een do what I please.*

The DIALOGUE.

Johnny. **W**HAT ails the foolish Woman,
  I think thou'lt be rul'd by no Man;
Is any thing more common,
  The Jarring in *Kirk* and State:
Gibby. That, *Johnny* has undone ye,
  Weez ne'er get a sock of Money,
  And ere worse Plagues light on ye,
  To *Scotland* Ise gang my gate.
    Folk by the Ears are a falling, falling,
    Folly and Mischief are bawling, bawling;
    Hey marry where's the Peace,
    How mun I do to lig here at Ease?
Johnny. Look to your Butter ye Jade, and Cheese.

If

If thou dost prate of Ruin,
Each Party has long been brewing,
What this mad World is doing,
Be sure thou wilt feel the Lash ;
Gibby. I've got a Stinging matter,
That over the Town I'll scatter,
Gud feth a bonny Satyr,
Oh how it shall Cut and Slash.
Johnny. Hussy, some Spy may be near us, near us,
Lyons have Ears, and may hear us, hear us ;
Not for your Life so bold,
Least the blind Justice hard by, be told.
Gibby. Deel o' my Saul, I can hardly hold.

Johnny. Our Foes have long been Humbling,
And one another Mumbling,
But now we must have our Grumbling,
And a very bold Assault ;
Gibby. Well *Johnny*, if th' Occasion,
Of Peace, can serve the Nation,
Let Union be in Fashion,
Tho' gud I dant like the Mault.
Johnny. Silence ye Baggage, no Prattle, prattle,
Kiss me, weez have a brisk Bottle, bottle,
Gibby and I wont part, Love's too well settled,
so soon to start,
Gibby. *Johnny* weel knows how to win my Heart.

A Politick Dialogue *between a Noble Lord belonging to the* ——— *Club, and his fine Lady: Concerning the late publick Rumour of the Q—ns Sickness, and Death at* Windsor. *The Words made to a Pretty Ayre.*

MY Dear, I've sent the Letter,
  I never yet wrote a better,
You hear how People scatter
  Abroad the good *Windsor* News ;
My Fortune I'll advance so,
And baulk the Tricks of *France* too,
I'll make the Lady Dance too,
  When she shall my Lines Peruse.

Lady.

As you have done, I have Penn'd another,
Ready dispatcht to her Grace, my Mother,
Who I am sure wont Cry,
She'll take a Dram that shall Grief defy ;

Lord.

All our whole *Club* too, are Drunk for Joy.

The Honest HIGHLANDER'S *new Health to the* QUEEN : *Occasion'd by a Debauch made by some Members of a certain Club, upon hearing of the late Lying News of Her Majesties Sickness and Death, the Words Made and Set to a pretty* SCOTCH *Ayre.*

Jockey. FRiend *Sawney* come sit near me,
   And lend me thy Luggs to hear me,
Thou hast no cause to fear me,
   Like some of the Loons I know ;
Ise tell thee sike a Story
Gud feth I'm wondrous sorry,
To find that *Britains* Glory,
   Should knavishly dwindle so :
News was of late the gud Q — n was Dying,
Spread by the —— and their Partys lying ;
When we should Wail and Cry,
Then our Crew were all Drunk for Joy.

They scrawl'd a Thousand Letters,
Containing doleful Matters,
Our Ministry in Fetters,
   Were all to receive their Dues ;
They hop'd to have a Chance too,
To baffle the Peace with *France* too,
And make the Lady Dance too,
   When she should their Lines peruse :
But on a sudden the Talk was over,
Providence did Royal *ANN* recover ;
Winter brings on the Green,
Agues then Physick are for a Q — n.

Then spite of their Endeavour,
That Loyal Zeal would sever,
Live, live oh Queen, for ever !
   In Glory without Eclipse ;

The

The Vipers here all routed
E're long will be, ne'er doubt it,
As *Teagueland* have out-voted,
    The Baiters of Honest *Phipps:*
In the mean while tho' base Humour ranges,
We're not Ambitious of Foreign changes ;
Drink then a Health Sublime,
Flourish Great *ANN*, to the end of Time.
    Flourish Great ANN, to the end of Time.

The FOX-*Hunter :*

A Song *in my New Comedy of the* Bath.

AWAY, ye brave *Fox* hunting Race,
    Away, away to a bourn Chace ;
Let *Ashton* Park alone to Day,
For here will be the Royal Play :
See yonder's the Covert, to Horse let's be going,
Throw, throw off the finders then, honest *Will. Owen.*
    Away ye brave, &c.   [*Bugles sound.*

Unkennel quick, yon blaky Ground,
They'll have a touch for Fifty Pound ;
Hark, hark to *Soundwell*, thats a noble Dog,
Cross him my Jolly Lads, heux, heux the Drag :
The *Fox* has broke Covert, let none lag behind,
We've had an Entappesse, she runs up the Wind ;
    Off with the Chace Hounds hoa,
    Now, now the Sportsmen shew :
        Let *Lillywhore* and *Cæsar* run ;
            Tosspot and *Ruler*,
            Capper and *Cooler*,
        Pompey and *Gallant*, Low 'em on.

Spurr

Spurr, Switch, and then away, o'er Hedges, and
    Ditches,
Without fear of Necks, or Gauling your Breeches :
Blow a Retreat blow, blow, Tantivee, tivee, tivee, tivee,
If she runs down the Wind she may chance to deceive
    ye* ;
A Recheat, a Recheat, Tivee, tivee, tivee, tivee,
Pox on't we're baulk'd, for by my Soul,
The vixen's just now Earth'd, see here's the Hole ;
Put in the Tarriers, Faith 'tis so,
She's crept at least five Yards below ;
They're working, hark, and lay at her so well,
They'll make her bolt, tho 'twere as deep as Hell ;
'Tis done, 'tis done, she's snapp'd, she's kill'd,
Hollow brave Boys then from the Field,
And Jolly Huntsman blow poor *Reynards* Knell †.

---

* *Horns Sound again.*
† *Bugles sound the Death of the* Fox.

The Mistress: A New Song.

CHloe's a Nymph in flowry Groves,
    A *Nereid* in the Streams ;
Saint-like she in the Temple moves,
    A Woman in my Dreams.

Love steals Artillery from her Eyes,
    The *Graces* point her Charms ;
Orpheus is Rivall'd in her Voice,
    And *Venus* in her Arms.

Never so happily in one,
    Did Heaven and Earth combine ;
And yet 'tis Flesh and Blood alone,
    That makes her so Divine.

She

She looks indeed like other Dames,
  With *Atlas* cover'd o'er ;
But when undress'd she meets my Flames,
  A Mortal she's no more.

To a Lady that would allow all Favours, but One. A SONNET.

'TIS not a Kiss, or gentle Squeez,
    A Compliment or smiling Eye ;
That can my Anxious Bosom ease,
    Or quell the Flame that soars so high :
Each welcome Favour giving hope,
    Dear *Cælia* swell'd my Joys at first ;
But stinted is but like a drop
    That's given to one, that dies with Thirst.

Fool'd *Tantalus* in Days of Old,
    Had greatest Torment for his Sin,
Doom'd not to Taste, yet still behold
    The Fruit was bobbing at his Chin :
Such Luscious Plums, and Grapes I view,
    Whilst all by me are highly priz'd ;
Can you a Guest, Invited too,
    Think fit then should be Tantaliz'd.

Who lets his Friend but only sip
    His Wine, is Niggard of his store ;
So tho' I tast your Rosie Lip,
    'Tis nothing, if you grant no more :
With Fragments some the Stomach please,
    And small repast, the Humour fits ;
But Love's a Lord of Noble Race,
    And cannot Dine on Scraps and Bits.
                              DAMON'S

DAMON'*s Retirement.*

D*Amon* fond of his Peaceful retirement far from
the Town,
With sweet *Cloris* upon the fresh Bank of *Avon* sate
down :
Folding Arms there about her soft Neck, ye Pow'rs
Divine,
He cry'd, how vain are the Worlds gaudy Trifles
when *Chloris* is mine.

Poor

Poor *Augusta* each Hour thou survivest new Troubles
    still brings,
Tost and tumbled, and banded about, 'twixt *Senates* and
    Kings;
Time revolving thou ne'er art secure of what is thine,
Then ah, how happy am I? that am sure that dear
    Chloris is mine.

View the Court and the Rays that shine, they are dimm'd
    with a Cloud,
View the Country in spite of the Peace, complainings
    are loud;
View the City, they'll swear their unhappy Trades
    decline,
Then blest am I that can say, Health, a Bottle, and
    Chloris are mine.

Young GUSTAVUS, *or the King of* SWEDEN'S
Health: Dedicated to all the Swedish
Merchants in London. *To a March of
Mr.* Jeremy Clark's.

Sing the 1st, 8 lines to the 1st. Strain, and the rest to the last.

DRINK, my Boys, Drink and rejoyce,
　There never was this Hundred Years,
　　For *Europe* better Cause ;
　The *Czar* is maul'd,
　His Foxes hol'd,
In Shoals the Bears do fly :
　Tho' tis clear,
　His sneaking here,
Was slily to be taught of us the Policy of War :
Yet who'd have thought the Frantick Sot,
　Durst fall on our Ally :
　　But he's gone,
　　He's quite undone,
　His Money and Artillery the *Swede* has won;
French Measures now will fail,
And *Spanish* wont prevail,
This Action has turn'd the Scale ;
　　Follow then thou Flow'r of Men,
　　The Spirit of thy Ancestor revive again ;
And whilst they howl and rave,
A Bumper we will have,
A Health to Young *Gustave.*

An

An ALLEGORY.

Set to MUSICK *by Mr.* Henry Purcell.

A Grashopper, and a Fly,
    In Summer hot and dry,
In eager Argument were met,
    About, about Priority :

Says the Fly to the Grashopper,
    From mighty Race I spring,
Bright *Phœbus* was my Dad, 'tis known,
    And I Eat and Drink with a King.

Says the Grashopper to the Fly,
    Such Rogues are still, still preferr'd ;
Your Father might be of high Degree,
    But your Mother was but a Turd, a Turd, a Turd.

CHORUS.

CHORUS.

So Rebel *Jemmy Scot,*
So Rebel *Jemmy Scot,*
  That did to Empire soar ;
His Father might be the Lord knows what,
His Father might be the Lord knows what,
  But his Mother we knew a whore, a whore, a whore,
    a whore, a whore, a whore, a whore, a whore ;
His Father might be the Lord knows what,
  But his Mother we knew a whore, a whore, a whore,
    a whore.

A

An ODE

On the QUEEN'S *Birth-day.*

'TIS gone, the Black and Gloomy Year,
  When *Britain* her sad Sables wore,
And Bright *Urania* with a Tear,
Saluted every dawning Hour,
Whilst Sorrow Triumph'd o'er her Rest,
And Joy was Stranger to her Breast.

Then welcome to the Rising Sun,
New usher'd by the Blushing Morn,
That now her Birth-day has begun,
To give us Comfort in our turn ;
This, after Woe, Heaven Joy assigns,
This, after-Tempest *Phœbus* Shines.

Urania then for ever Live,
The Joy of Hearts, and *England's* Bliss,
Whose Virtues only can retrieve,
Our long-griev'd Nation's Happiness,
And Render to each Mourning Muse,
The Treasures they so late did lose.

Ye happy Nine now chant your Lays,
Joyn Instruments with Voices Right;
This Day in Tuneful numbers Praise,
That brought *Urania* to the Light,
The Soul of Arts and Sciences,
And Charming Musick's Patroness.

Good, tho' in this Corrupted Time,
When Vice has such Aluring Ways,
Humble, tho' by Descent Sublime,
As Providence had Power to raise,
Pious as Angels, Kind to the Distrest,
Bane to the bad, and Pattern to the best.

Oh !

Oh! that as here our Beauteous Thames,
Profound and smoothly flows along,
I could in clear Poetick Streams,
Raise to Fames highest Pitch my Song,
Since lov'd *Urania* is the Theam,
Unblasted Vertue in Extream.

Then would she most wondrous things,
Nature is doing and has done,
Of forming Heroes Infant Kings,
Theams for fam'd Bards to write upon,
I'd Sing of *England's* Royal Bud,
Fated for our hereafter Good.

That lovely Plant which now does shoot,
In fibious Twigs and Branches small,
Will when full Grown and fix'd at Root,
Protect from storms and shade us all,
Whilst highly we Heaven's Gift Esteem,
And bless *Urania's* Name for him.

For ever then upon this Day,
Apollo shew thy Glorious Face,
Grant every Muse a Golden Ray,
Whilst such Exalted worth they Praise,
And still thro' Ages all along,
Urania be the Poet's Song.

A PINDARICK ODE, *On* NEW-YEAR's-DAY : *Perform'd by Voca l and Instrumental Musick, before their* SACRED MAJESTIES *K.* WILLIAM *and* Q. MARY.

Set by Dr. JOHN BLOW.

Matutine pater, seu Jane *libentius audis,*
Unde homines operum primos, vitaque labores
Instituunt, (sic Dis placitum) tu Carminis esto
Principium,——   Horace.

BEHOLD, how all the Stars give way ;
  Behold, how the revolving Sphere,
Swells to bring forth the Sacred Day ;
That ushers in the Mighty Year ;
Whilst *Janus* with his double Face
Viewing the present Time and past,
In strong Prophetick Fury sings,
Our Nation's Glory and our King's.

See *England's* Genius, like the dazling Sun,
Proud of his Race, to our Horizon run
To welcome that Cælestial Power,
That of this Glorious Year begins the Happy Hour :
  A Year from whence shall Wonders come ;
  A Year to baffle *France* and *Rome*,
  And bound the dubious Fate of Warring *Christendom*.

Move on with Fame, all ye Triumphant Days,
To *Britain's* Honour, and to *Cæsar's* Praise ;
Let no short Hour of this Year's bounded Time,
Pass by without some Act sublime :
Great WILLIAM, Champion of the Mighty States,
And all the Princes the Confederates :
Ploughs the Green *Neptune*, whilst to waft him o'er,
The Fates stand smiling on the *Belgick* Shoar :

                                        And

And now the *Gallick* Genius Trembles,
How e'er she Pannick Fear dissembles ;
To know the Mighty League, and view the Mighty
Pow'r.

So when the *Persian* Pride of old,
Disdain'd their God the Sun,
With Armies and more powerful Gold,
Did half the World o'er-run,
Brave *Alexander* chang'd their Scorn to Awe,
And came, and Fought, and Conquer'd like *NASSAU.*

Then welcome Wondrous Year,
More Happy and Serene,
Than any ever did appear,
To bless *Great Cæsar* and his Queen :
May every Hour encrease their Fames ;
Whilst Ecchoing Skies resound their Names :
And when Unbounded Joy, and the Excess
Of all that can be found in Humane Bliss,
Fall on 'em, may each Year be still like this,
Health, Fortune, Grandeur, Fame, and Victory,
And Crowning all, a Life, long as Eternity.

CHORUS.

Come ye Sons of Great Apollo,
Let your charming Consorts follow ;
Sing of Triumph, sing of Beauty,
Sing soft Ayres of Loyal Duty;
Give to Cæsar's *Royal Fair*
Songs of Joy to Calm her Care,
Bid the less Auspicious Year adieu,
And give her joyful Welcomes to the New.

The

The HAPPY MAN,

A SONG.   *The Words made to a pretty Tune.*

Whilst abroad Renown and Glory,
    Are Mankind diminishing ;
A Fate, a rugged Master,
    Still decides the Strife :
To swell our future Story,
    When the VVar is finishing,
How this and that Disaster,
    Cost many a Heroes Life ;
        With a Book in Contemplation,
        In a Corner of the Nation,
        In a Bower of Bliss,
        Near a Grove of Trees,
VVhere a Brook runs purling down :
        VVith a Conscience free,
        A Friendly he,
        And one kind she,
        That's true to me,
And hates the noisy Town :
        For VVrong or Right,
        Let Nations Fight,
        My chief Delight,
        Shall be Content alone.

OLD Tony,

A SONG.   The Tune, *How happy is*
PHILLIS *in Love.*

L Et *Oliver* now be forgotten,
   His Policy's quite out of Doors;
Let *Bradshaw* and *Hewson* lie rotten,
   Like Sons of *Fanatical* VVhores:
For *Tony's* grown a Patrician,
By Voting Damn'd Sedition,
      For many Years
      Fam'd Politician,
The Mouth of all *Presbyter*-Peers.

Old

Old *Tony* a Turn-coat at *Worc'ster,*
   Yet swore he'd maintain the King's Right ;
But *Tony* did swagger and bluster,
   Yet never drew Sword on his side ;
For *Tony's* like an old Stallion,
He has still the Pox of Rebellion,
     And never was sound,
     Like the *Camelion,*
Still changing his Shape and his Ground.

Old *Rowley's* return'd (Heav'ns bless Him)
   From Exile and danger set free :
Old *Tony* made haste to address Him;
   And swore none more Loyal than he :
The King who knew him a Traytor,
And saw him Squint like a Satyr ;
     Yet, thro' his Grace,
     Pardon'd the matter,
And gave him since the *Purse* and the *Mace.*

And now little Chancellor *Tony*
   VVith Honour had feather'd his VVing,
He carefully pick'd up the Money,
   But never a Groat for the King :
But *Tony's* luck was confounded,
The Duke soon smoak'd him a *Round-head,*
     From Head to Heel
     Tony was sounded,
And great *York* put a Spoke in his VVeel.

And now little *Tony* in Passion,
 . Like Boy that had nettl'd his Breech,
Maliciously took an occasion
   To make a most delicate Speech ;
He told the King like a Croney,
If e'er he hop'd to have Money,
     He must be rul'd :
     Oh fine *Tony !*
Was ever Potent Monarch so school'd ?

                    The

The King issues out Proclamation
  By Learned and Loyal Advice ;
But *Tony* possesses the Nation
  The Councel will never be wise :
For *Tony* is madder and madder,
And *Monmouth's* blown like a Bladder,
    And *L——ce* too,
    Who grows gladder,
That they the great *York* were like to subdue.

But Destiny shortly will cross it,
  For *Tony's* grown Gouty and Sick ;
In Spight of his Spiggot and Fawset,
  The States-man must go to old *Nick :*
For *Tony* rails at the *Papist*,
Yet he himself is an *Atheist*,
    Tho' so precise,
    Foolish and Apish,
Like holy *Quack*, or *Priest* in disguise.

But now let this Rump of the Law see,
  A Maxim as Learned in part,
Whoe'er with his Prince is too sawcy,
  'Tis fear'd he's a Traytor in's Heart :
Then *Tony* cease to be witty
By buzzing Treason i'th' City,
    And love the King ;
    So ends my Ditty :
Or else maist thou die, like a Dog in a string.

The WHIGS EXALTATION.

To an old Tune of Forty One.

Now, now the *Tories* all shall stoop,
  Religion and the Laws,
And *Whigs* on *Commonwealth* get up,
  To Tap the *GOOD OLD CAUSE* :
Tantivy-boys shall all go down,
  And haughty *Monarchy*,
The *Leathern Cap* shall brave the *Throne*,
  Then hey Boys up go we !

When

When once that *Antichristian* Crew,
  Are crush'd and overthrown,
We'll teach their *Nobles* how to bow,
  And keep their *Gentry* down.
Good manners has a bad repute,
  And tends to Pride we see;
We'll therefore cry all Breeding down,
  Then hey Boys up go we.

The name of Lord shall be abhorr'd,
  For ev'ry Man's a Brother;
What reason then in *Church* or *State*
  One Man should rule another?
Thus having peel'd and plunder'd all,
  And levell'd each degree,
We'll make their plump young Daughters fall,
  And hey Boys up go we.

VVhat tho' the *King* and *Parliament*
  Cannot accord together,
VVe have good cause to be content
  This is our Sun-shine weather;
For if good *Reason* shou'd take place,
  And they should both agree,
'Dzounds wou'd be in a *Round-head's* case;
  For hey then up go we.

VVe'll down with all the '*Versities*
  VVhere *Learning* is profest:
For they still Practice and Maintain,
  The *Language of the Beast;*
VVe'll Exercise in every Grove,
  And Preach beneath a Tree,
VVe'll make a *Pulpit* of a *Tub,*
  Then hey Boys up go we.

The *Whigs* shall rule *Committe-chair,*
  VVho will such Laws invent,
As shall Exclude the Lawful *Heir*
  By *Act of Parliament:*

VVe'll

VVe'll cut his *Royal Highness* down,
 Ev'n shorter by the *Knee,*
That he shall never reach the *Throne,*
 Then hey Boys up go we.

VVe'll smite the *Idol* in *Guild-Hall,*
 And then (as we were wont,)
VVe'll cry it was a *Popish-Plot,*
 And swear those Rogues have don't,
His Royal Highness to Unthrone
 Our Interest will be,
For if he e'er enjoy his own
 Then hey Boys up go we.

VVe'll break the VVindows which the VVhore
 Of *Babylon* has painted ;
And when their *Bishops* are pull'd down,
 Our *Elders* shall be *Sainted :*
Thus having quite enslav'd the *Throne,*
 Pretending to set free,
At length the *Gallows* claims its own,
 Then hey Boys up go we.

To the KING:

An ODE *on his Birth-Day.*

CLowdy *Saturnia* drives her Steeds apace,
  Heaven-born *Aurora* presses to her place ;
And all the new-dress'd Planets of the Night,
Dance their gay Measures with unusual Grace,
  To usher in the happy Morning's Light,
  To usher in, &c.

Now blest *Britannia*, let thy Head be crown'd,
Now let thy joyful Trumpets sound ;
  Into the late enslav'd **Augusta's* Ears,   * *London.*
The Triumphs of a Day renown'd :
  Beyond the Glories of all former Years,
A Day when Eastern Kings to kneel forbore,
  And end the Worship they begun ;
Dazl'd with rising Glories from the *British* Shore,
  No longer they ador'd the Sun.
Chorus. A Day when, *&c.*

[*Second Movement.*]
  The *Belgick* Sages saw from far
  The glittering Regal Star,
  That blest the happy Morn,
  When great *Nassau* was born:
  They heard besides a Cherub sing,
    Haste, haste without delay,
    To *Albion* haste away,
  Revenge their Wrongs, and be a King :
  Before thy Sword, and awful Frown,
  Rome's Pagan Gods shall tumble down ;
  Haste to oppose *Britannia's* Foes,
  And then to wear her Crown.
  And now the Day is come,
  So dreadful to Proud *Rome* ;

The Day when *Gallia* shakes,
And *England's* Genius wakes ;
To call her Sons to fight,
And guard **Eusebia's* Right ;   * *The Church.*
  Hark, hark, I hear their loud Alarms,
And what was sold for tempting Gold,
  Retriev'd again by Arms.
Chorus. Guard, guard *Eusebia's* Right,
Call, call her Sons to fight ;
  Hark, hark, *&c.*

[*Third Movement.*]

Go on, admir'd *Nassau*, go on,
To Fame and Victory go on,
  Recover *Britain's* long lost Glory ;
Reflect on former Battles won,
And what by *English* Monarchs done,
  In *Edward's* and Great *Henry's* Story ;
Whilst we in lofty Song, and tuneful Mirth,
Each Year sing loud, to Celebrate his Birth ;
Whom bounteous Heaven, with Paternal Hand,
Sent as a Second Saviour to this groaning Land.

CHORUS of all.

  on, *let thy Joy appear,*
  Restor'd is now thy happy State;
The greatest Blessings are most dear,
  When we atchieve 'em late:
And whilst in a Jubilee Triumph we sing,
All Hail, Great Nassau, *all Joy to the King,*
Let a Chorus of Thunder in the loud Consort play,
To inform the vast Globe this is Cæsar's *Birth-Day.*

The BANDITTI :

Ban. 1. THE Joys of Court, or City,
　　The Fame of Fair, or Witty,
Are Toys to the *Banditti*,
　Whilst our Cups we drein ;
Ban. 2. We love, we laugh, we lie here,
We eat, we drink, we die here,
And valiantly defie here,
　All the Power of *Spain.*

But when by our Scout, a Prize we find,
We all run out to seize him,
Stand, stand we cry, or ye Dog, ye die,
　Without any more ado ;
All this brings us no Slander,
Each Conquering great Commander,
And mighty *Alexander*,
　Were *Banditties* too.

Ban. 1. Some we bind, and some we gag,
Some we strip and plunder,
Some that have store of Gold,
　Into our Cave we draw ;
Thus like first moulded Matter,
Our Principles we scatter,
'Twas Folly made good Nature,
　And Fear that first made Law.

Ban.

Ban. 2. And when we come home, our Doxies run,
To bid us kindly Welcome,
Plump, Fresh, and Young, all down do lye
    On Beds of Moss, to Sport ;
Thus every valiant Ranger,
Lies at rack and Manger,
And he that's past most Danger,
    Has most Kisses for't.

Ban. Fools do whine, and sigh, and pine,
Fools fall sick of Fevers,
Fools doat on fleeting Joys,
    That oft does Ruin bring ;
Whilst without begging Pity
Of the Wise, the Fair, or Witty,
The Brave, the bold *Banditti*,
    Has the self-same thing.

Sir Rob. Bedingfeild *the Lord-Mayor's Health.*

M Ounsieur now disgorges fast
The Towns were lately won ;
Cloudy Days clear up at last,
The Crust is off the Sun :

Brit.

Brittish Heroes prove they can,
  Their former Credit raise ;
Conqu'ring now for glorious *ANN*,
  As in great *Henry's* Days :
Marlbrough and renown'd *Eugene*
Inspir'd by our Auspicious Queen :
    The *Empire* late did save,
    To *Savoy* Freedom gave,
    Which makes Old *Bourbon* rave,
    That meant it to enslave,
'Twill punish him with Death,
  Beyond the Grave.

Great *Augusta* † fill thy Baggs,   † *London.*
  And revel in thy Furrs ;
Since with Conquest glorious Flaggs,
  Free happy Trade concurs :
Italy and *Flanders* now,
  Ope' wide their Gates to Peace ;
Spain and th' *Indies* soon must bow,
  And Wealth from all increase.
Jarrs no more shall Plague the Town,
The *Kirk* no more pull Steeples down ;
    Then cease all needless Fear
    Or Doubts, the coming Year,
    And brimming Bowls prepare,
    For all true Hearts to share,
    A joyful Health to him that fills the Chair.

BARTHOLOMEW-FAIR, *a Catch: Set to Musick by Dr.* JOHN BLOW.

H ERE is the Rarity of the whole *Fair*,
    Pimper-le-pimp, and the wise Dancing Mare ;
Here's valiant St. *George* and the *Dragon*, a Farce,
A Girl of Fifteen with strange Moles on her A—.

Here is *Vienna* Besieg'd, a Rare thing,
And here's *Punchinello* shown thrice to the King ;
Then see the Masks to the *Cloister* repair,
But there will be no Raffling, a Pox take the May'r,

A CATCH *set by Doctor* BLOW.

I N a Seller at *Sodom*, at the Sign of the T—,
  Two buxom young Harlots were drinking with *L*— ;
Some say they were his Daughters, no matter for that,
They're resolv'd they would souse their old Dad with
    a Pot :
All fluster'd and bousie, the Doting old Sot,
As great as a Monarch between 'em was got ;
Till the Eldest and Wisest thus open'd the Plot,
Pray shew us dear Daddy how we were begot :
Godzoukes, you young Jades,'twas the first Oath I wot,
The Devil of a Serpent this Humour has taught ;
No matter, they cry'd, you shall Pawn for the shot,
Unless you will shew us how we were begot.

A

A SONG.

THERE's such Religion in my Love,
      It must like Vertue have Reward;
And *Strephon's* Faith will from above,
      Tho' not below, find due regard:

Tell

Tell me no more of Friends or Foes,
  That hinder'd what your Heart design'd ;
No Parents can your Love dispose,
  No more than they beget your Mind.

Great *Love !* the Monarch of our Wills,
  When I am lost by your Disdain ;
Will doom that Scorn your Lovers kills,
  To be your fatal Beauty's bane :
You, like a Bee, has stung my Heart,
  Yet there the avenging Dart does lye ;
Which gives you in my Fate a part,
  And you are undone as well as I.

CHORUS.

K IND Heaven no Peace to the Perjur'd allows,
    In Fate's gloomy Book keeps account of all
        Vows ;
And *Jove* that does view the false and the true,
Knows who kept their Promise, and who deceiv'd who :
Will swear by the Skies, and *Ganimede's* Eyes,
No Woman that mingles Affection with Art ;
And here in the Farce of the World plays a part,
Shall ever hereafter, shall ever hereafter,
Shall ever hereafter break a fond Heart,
Shall ever hereafter break a fond Heart.

To pretty Mrs. H. D. *upon the sight of her Picture standing amongst others at* Mr. *Knellers.*

*C*Orrinna when you left the Town,
    My Heart secure I thought to find;
But found alas new Chains put on,
    By your bright Image left behind.

Your Picture now the Conquest has,
    To my fond Soul new Flame returns;
Like Rays contracted in a Glass,
    Though distant, your Reflection burns.

Had Paradise for you been lost,
    Like *Adam* I had suffer'd too;
What must that Fruit be to the Taste,
    That is so Tempting to the View.

Your Graces shining at full length,
    Subdue each Souls devotest Skill;
When Beauty Charms beyond our Strength,
    Where is the use of our Free-Will?

Like that Astronomer I gaze,
    That his propitious Star had found;
Fixing my Eyes upon your Face,
    I slight the glittering Planets round.

And as to Shrines when Pilgrims go,
    Such awful Reverence I feel,
That though I'm sure 'tis only show,
    I scarcely can forbear to kneel.

The

The SHUTTLECOCK:

A New SONG, *Set to a pretty* SCOTCH *Tune by Mr.* Courtiville.

HAVE you seen Battledore play,
    Where the Shuttlecock flys to and fro One?
Or, have you noted an *April* day, now Raining,
Now Shining, now warming, now Storming?
    Ah! just, just such as these is a Woman.

Love and true Merit do seldom prevail,
For always we hold a wet Eel by the Tail;
Their Tongues ne'er are Idle, the Humour's a Riddle,
They prick with their Needle, and ogle and wheedle;
    And if they have Charms,
Tis rarely that Beauty is true t'ye,
For few or none you are sure are your own,
    But in your Arms.

A

A Song *upon Mrs.* Brace-girdle's *Acting*
Marcella, *in* Don-Quixote.   *Set by Mr.*
Fingar.

W Hile I with wounding Grief did look,
    When Love had turn'd your Brain ;
From you the dire Disease I took,
    And bore my self your pain,

Marcella

Marcella then your Lover prize,
  And be not too severe ;
Use well the Conquests of your Eyes,
  For Pride has cost ye Dear.

Ambrosio treats your Flames with scorn,
  And racks your tender Mind ;
Withdraw your Frowns, and Smiles return,
  And pay him in his kind.

Yet Smile again where Smiles are due,
  And my true Love esteem ;
For I much more do rage for you,
  Than you can burn for him.

Love's Revenge. A SONG.

THE World was hush'd, and Nature lay
  Lull'd in a soft Repose ;
As I in Tears reflecting lay
  On *Chloe's* faithless Vows :
The God of Love all gay appear'd,
  To heal my wounded Heart ;
New pangs of Joy my Soul indear'd,
  And pleasure charm'd each part :
Fond Man, said he, here end thy Woe,
Till they my Power and Justice know,
The foolish Sex will all do so.

But for thy Ease believe, no Bliss
  Is perfect without Pain ;
The fairest Summer hurtful is
  Without some Showers of Rain :
The Joys of Heaven, who would prize,
  If Men too cheaply bought ;
The dearest part of Mortal Joys,
  Most charming is when sought :

And though with Dross true Love they pay,
Those that know finest Metal say,
No Gold will Coyn without allay.

But that the Generous Lover may,
  Not always sigh in vain ;
The Cruel Nymph that kills to Day,
  To-morrow shall be slain :
The little God no sooner spoke,
  But from my sight he flew ;
And I that groan'd with *Chloe's* Yoke,
  Found Love's Revenge was true:
Her proud hard Heart too late did turn
With fiercer Flames than mine did burn,
Whilst I as much began to scorn.

The Moralist.   *A* SONG.

WHAT's the worth of Health or Living,
  If we stint our selves of Bliss ;
Grief is but a self-deceiving,
  Chusing may be for what is :
Dos'd all Night, and daily weeping,
  Zealots think to Heaven to climb ;
Thus with Canting and with Sleeping,
  The poor Sots lose all their Time.

Give me Love, and give me Wine too,
  For Life's Cares to make amends ;
Wit and Poetry Divine too,
  And a charming Female Friend :
In a Moral honest Station,
  To my Grave in Peace I'll go ;
Let the bug *Predestination,*
  Fright the Fools no better know.

To

To CYNTHIA.

A SONG.

BORN with the Vices of my kind,
   I were Inconstant too ;
Dear *Cynthia*, could I rambling find
   More Beauty than in you.

The rowling Surges of my Blood,
   By Virtue now ebb'd low ;
Should a new Shower encrease the Flood,
   Too soon would overflow.

But Frality when thy Face I see,
   Does modestly retire ;
Uncommon must her Graces be,
   Whose look can bound desire.

Not to my Virtue, but thy Power,
   This Constancy is due ;
When change it self can give no more,
   'Tis easie to be true.

The two following SONGS, *Sung in my Play*
call'd, the Commonwealth of Women.

Liberty's the Soul of Living,
  Ev'ry hour new Joys receiving ;
No sharp Pangs our Hearts are grieving,
  Liberty's the Soul of Living :
Here are no false Men presuming,
  Youth or Beauty to its Ruin ;
Murm'ring Sighs, like Turtles cooing,
  Nor the bitter Sweets of wooing.

C H O R U S.

CHORUS.

Then since we are doom'd to be Chast,
And Loving is counted a Crime;
Let's do what we can, not to think of a Man,
But make the best use of our Prime.

A Song.

Ynthia with an awful Power,
   On all Hearts extends her sway ;
Did the Eastern Natives know her,
   They'd less prise the God of Day :
On her Brow Night shady lies,
   Whilst Morning breaks from her fair Eyes ;
On her Brow Night shady lies,
   Whilst Morning breaks from her fair Eyes.

An

An ODE.

From ANACREON.

IF Gold could lengthen Life, I swear,
  It then should be my chiefest Care;
To get a heap, that I may say,
When Death came to Demand his Pay,
Thou Slave, take this, and go thy way.

But since Life is not to be bought,
  Why should I plague my self for nought,
Or foolishly disturb the Skies,
With vain Complaints, or fruitless Cries,
For if the fatal Destinies
  Have all decreed it shall be so,
  What good will Gold or Crying do.

Give me to ease my thirsty Soul,
  The Joys and Comforts of the Bowl;
Freedom and Health, and whilst I live,
Let me not want what Love can give:
Then shall I die in Peace, and have
This Consolation in the Grave,
That once I had the World my Slave.

The Old Fumbler.

A SONG: *Set by Mr.* Hen. Purcell.

Smug, rich and fantastick old Fumbler was known,
    That Wedded a Juicy brisk Girl of the Town;
Her Face like an Angel, Fair, Plump, and a Maid,
Her Lute well in Tune too, cou'd he but have plaid :
But lost was his Skill, let him do what he can,
She finds him in Bed a weak silly old Man ;
He coughs in her Ear, 'tis in vain to come on,
Forgive me, my Dear, I'm a silly old Man.

She laid his dry Hand on her snowy soft Breast,
And from those white Hills gave a glimpse of the Best ;
But ah ! what is Age when our Youth's but a Span,
She found him an Infant instead of a Man,
Ah ! Pardon, he'd cry, that I'm weary so soon,
You have let down my Base, I'm no longer in Tune ;
Lay by the dear Instrument, prithee lie still,
I can play but one Lesson, and that I play Ill.

An

Orations, Poems, Prologues, *and* Epilogues *on several Occasions.*

An ORATION,

Address'd to the PRINCE *and* PRINCESS; *and spoken to divert the Nobility and my Friends, by me; upon the Publick Stage at the* Theatre, May 27, 1717.

AS some stout Warriour Valour to advance,
From fate has long had glorious Circumstance,
* Finding another Cause, tho' Years enlarge,
By Honour fir'd, resolves again to charge:
So I, that late my happy Verse did raise,
And with your generous Favour made Essays;
Oblig'd by your indulgent Grace before,
And blest by Time, Address to speak once more.

† Sovereign Remarks then my first Theam shall be,
A Monarch's Instance must take Place with me:
All kingly Mysterys are nicely shewn,
Yet still I hope they will my Candor own,
Who keep State Places, or who lay 'em down.
Shine then my Muse, with Radiance like the Sun,
That I may blaze some Acts by *Cæsar* done:
First, The dear Clemency to that bad Race,
Who durst deserve his God-like Act of Grace:
Then let the Triple-league be understood,
So greatly signal for the Kingdom's Good;
As if he meant, surmounting humane Praise,
T'o'ermatch the Zenith of Great *William's* Days.

Yet

* *The Poet's Remarks on himself.* † *Remarks on the King, and those that have left their Places.*

* Yet tho' his Royal Absence gave us Pain,
We must admire the Prince's happy Reign ;
Whose awful Sway prov'd so divinely well,
The want of *Cæsar* we could scarcely tell :
And prov'd, tho' warm'd in Youth's propitious Prime,
The Sence of fifty Years, in half the Time.

Yet Fate, alas'! that points not always fair,
Had nearly finish'd his indulgent Care ;
† The charming Princess, Soul of Beauty's Grace,
Joy of his Heart, and all our loyal Race,
Near Death was drawn —— But oh, no more of that,
Apollo sacred o'er the Palace sate,
The Muses a rejoycing Consort give,
And *Esculapius* brought the grand Reprieve :
Then from the dark Abyss succeeding Light came on,
And from her black Eclipse again divinely *Cynthia* shon ;
For her the dreadful Winter fiercely binds ;
For her came Frosts and bleak tempestuous Winds :
But when she heal'd, Earth did new Order bring,
And by her Graces form'd came in the Spring.

‖ *Albion* shall now no more *Pretenders* try,
Transported with her heavenly Progeny ;
For as some Desart Land, whose wild Distress
Seem'd wanting Providential Care to bless ;
Where the coy Sun ne'er darts a genial Ray,
But stormy Snows blast each returning Day :
Prayers of some favour'd Objects, shipwreck'd there,
Having with pious Toyl exacted heavenly Care :
Great Goddess, Nature, proving kindly Force,
Turns to proliffick Heat their steril Course.
So *Frederick*, with his Sisters, heavenly fair,
Where'er they move perfume the Ambient Air.

Oh

---

* *On the Prince.* † *On the Princess.* ‖ *On her Royal Family.*

* Oh Beauty! lend my *Autumn* thy Support,
How shall I else do Right to yon bright Court?
Exalt th' Inspirers that direct my Tongue,
And give me all the Flame that charms my Song;
Exert your Grace, each bright Angelick Power,
Disperse your Beams, Oh spread your sacred Store,
For if you cease to smile, I am no more.

† Each Goddess thus I leave in her Degree,
And now descend to you the Beaus Esprits,
A bold Invasion threatned your Estates,
Fierce Bug-bears bound, to fright our Candidates
Resolv'd in Jerkins buff, and black Cravats.

This fruitful Land strange foreign Foes will haunt,
Some lanch to fight for Fame, and some for Want;
Wild, Crack-brain'd Hotspurs too fierce Quarrels breed,
Like the mad Pagod of the North, the *Swede;*
From whose Excursions, tho' he toil with Pains
And fights, and flys, his Head small Plaud it gains,
The *Russian* got Dominion of his Brains;
Besides, our Ladies here have Scorn design'd,
For he's so barb'rous, he hates Woman-kind:
Thus Angel Amazons to War will go,
The very Devil *to them is not so great a Foe.*

|| To vary Subjects, News is next design'd,
News, that into a Sweat puts half Mankind;
The *Whig* and *Tory* must be here enroll'd,
Two Names that fright the Town with being told,
Worse than the *Guelphs,* and *Gibellins* of old.
The City Tribe with State Effects are stor'd,
And every Coffee-Room's a Councel-board:
The Taylor with grub Beard and Crimson Nose,
The King and Parliament together sows;

The

The snip-snap Barber, lathering Spain's *Condition,*
Affirms the League not good as the Partition :
The Cutler *swears, more Troops well-arm'd should meet,*
The Crop-ear'd Crispin *stitches up the Fleet ;*
Apollo's *only Race unbyass'd joyn,*
Whose loyal Hearts wish Britain's *Fame, like mine.*

As Spots in Stars, so Faults in Wit may be,
But Faction and rebellious Villany,
Ne'er taints the soaring Muse, aloft she sings,
On Theams of Glory, and great Deeds of Kings.

And now to end, since Spring has spread her Bloom,
And welcome Summer to endear is come ;
Since on our Sea each gawdy Streamer soars,
And the stout Army guards our happy Shores ;
Like my blest Genius, fated to oppose,
Oh let your Union joyn to rout our Foes.

* Then let the *Goths* and *Vandals* dare invade,
Let *Rome* and *Sicily* advance their Aid ;
Let the Grand Minister, to *Plimouth* sent,
Obstructed and imur'd, new Plots invent ;
Let him his witty Treasons there make good,
Get Freedom by a second Riding-hood.

Great *Britain*, whilst its Genius keeps her Shore,
To seize all Traytors shall exert its Power,
So guard the King, and *Albion's* Isle, 'till time shall
     be no more.

---

* *On the* Swede's *late Minister ; with a concluding*
Note on the King and Prince.

An

An ORATION,

Address'd to the Prince *and* Princess *of* Wales, *and the* Court; *Spoken by me at a great Audience at the* Theatre Royal *in* Drury Lane, May 29, 1716.

When *Britain's* prosperous Fortune was decay'd,
And *France* oblig'd by the late Peace we made,
Controuling Fate a mighty Death decreed,
To puzle all the Mischief should succeed :
Then our propitious Genius rose, and far
Brought from the *German* Regions prone to War,
The gracious Aid of mighty *Hanover :*
But his bright Foot had scarcely touch'd our Land,
And blest the Soil which nauseous Error stain'd ;
But the North Crew would do our Nation Right,
Loons bred in craggy Cliffs, but yet could fight :
Who o'er their Targets did a General gain,
Who was the Devil for Backsword, and for Brain ;
At *Preston* too, they made a bold Essay,
Two Seasons had, the Kingdom to dismay,
Yielded the first, the last, they ran away.
Among themselves let them that Grandeur right,
Success gave Trophies to our Monarch's Might,
Who did the Fate of his new Reign disclose,
And prove th' inervate Weakness of his Foes.
His Troops but view'd, could poor Insulters aw,
'Tis Fate enough to see the Lyon's Claw.
So when *Jove's* Thunder does the Globe alarm,
Vile Creatures fly to holes, and 'scape the harm,
Dissolv'd with fear of the Ætherial Storm :
Thus then Rebellion fell, and thus the Race
Of Glorious *Cæsar* shall have awful Grace.
The *Persian* Sage, who finds when Morn comes on,
A dark Eclipse invade his God the Sun ;

Di-

Distorts his trembling Limbs, his Nerves are sore, }
Staring his Eyes, and cold his vital Gore,
As having never seen the like before :
But when the Orb is mov'd, and *Sol* appears,
The glimmering of brisk Light his Reason chears ;
He slights his Fear, and as the Sun displays,
Thinks it has given more Lustre to its Rays.
So mighty Sir,* you by this Tumult late, [* *The Prince.*
May timely reckon your Degrees of State ;
Some Treasons hoodwinkt, Fortune must infuse,
As Poysons are in Med'cines that we use :
But both in their exalted kind excel,
One brings ye Fame, as t'other makes ye well.
Glory thus finish'd, Beauty must ensue,
In state of which, Ladies† I bow to you ; [† *The Ladies.*
You, whose Divinity the Art does take,
To teach me how to write, and how to speak ;
The World's chief Blessing in its best Degree,
As Genius of what is, or is to be ;
Yet as some grave Astronomer that has
To search a Planet, found a noted Cause :
The Time in some Distress does form Degrees,
And in the Blaze a Speck disorder'd sees.
So tho' a dazling Lustre charms around,
A casual Speck within the Ray is found ;
A Graveness palls the *Cupid.*   Some don't use
To ask what Fashion's now ; but ask what News ?
What Projects? has no other Lady stood,
T'outwit the Court and Tower, nor Plot pursu'd ;
Has there been ne'er a second Riding-hood ?
Their Brains, instead of Billets, Treason quotes,
All am'rous Songs have lost their tuneful Notes,
And leaving sacred Verse, they read the Votes :
But oh, what Horror does our Passions draw,
When Ladies cease to charm, to model Church and
    Law.

And now ye sprightly Wits, ye modern Beaus,
That here descend from those Angelick Rows,

Some

Some of your Tenets late did faintly spring, ⎫
Which stanch Religion so deprav'd did bring, ⎬
Some would have lost it quite, with a New King; ⎭
Fresh Legislature had supply'd their Will,
And baulk'd the Force of our septennial Bill.

If fatal Mischiefs in our Isle commence,
We've still the starry Grace of Providence :
This shon when Patriots confirm'd in Grace,
All wise and loyal brought that Law to pass ;
When two to one the Kingdom's Good decreed,
And proud Rebellion dar'd, that durst succeed :
Oh, may they ever shine, who broke our civil Wars,
And Nature ceasing, blaze among the Stars.

Whene'er our Sovereign's Regal Genius soars,
And potent *Marlborough* leads his conqu'ring Powers,
Arch Rebels no Subversion here can breed, ⎫
The Regent's double Note we ne'er shall heed, ⎬
Nor fear the boisterous Navy of the *Swede.* ⎭

This glorious Theam, so tow'ring and sublime,
Inspir'd aloft, retrieves my fading Time ;
I think this Hour most happy to rehearse
Our Monarch's Character in tuneful Verse :
Mild, yet August, Goodness th' Almighty gave,
Just as his Laws, and without Passion brave.

On then, ye sovereign Party with Applause,
Fight for your sacred King, and sacred Cause ;
'Gainst all Pretenders let your Valour shine,
To strengthen *Cæsar* and his Sacred Line :

Whilst I, that in my former springing Hours, ⎫
Saw Plants without Produce, and wither'd Flowers, ⎬
When fatal Plots obstructed regal Powers, ⎭
Do in my plenteous, fruitful *Autumn* raise,
On *Albion's* Wealth and Fame triumphant Praise ;
And with due Fame of its Restorer sing,
Th' inspiring Annals of our glorious King.

The NITHISDALE:

Vulgarly call'd a Riding-hood. *A* POEM.
*On the sudden, Timely, and Incomparable
Purpose of the Countess of* Nithisdale;
*who frustrated the dreadful Judgment and
Sentence of the Lord High* Steward, *and
sav'd her Husband's Neck from the Block.*
Feb. 25, 1715.

OH every tuneful Bard that Sings,
 Of Ladies Wits and Ladies Things;
Of Moulding Face, or Teeth, or Hair,
Design'd to make 'em Young and Fair:
Let Iron Hoops not made for shew,
Nor Whale-bone Fardingales below,
No more in Praise be understood;
But now Exalt the Riding-hood,

Our Hats with Feathers they inclose,
Our Coats they wear, and ride like Beaus,
Our Breeches too they'll quickly find,
And set up then to Ape Mankind:
But since to take they are so bold
Our Cloaks, that shade from Rain and Cold,
I'll study now the Nation's good,
And thus Expose the Riding-hood.

It first does Cleanliness decay,
And proves a thousand Sluts a Day;
Their Linnen too all ill may be,
They hide it so, as none can see.
Then let the Husband, who with strife,
Perceives a Gallant loves his Wife;
Think 'tis for Cuckold-making good,
No cover like a Riding-hood.

Thus

Thus in our Days of Life 'twill raise,
A hundred Tricks, a hundred Ways ;
And now my Story to pursue,
You'll see what it in Death can do :
'Tis call'd a *Nithisdale*, since Fame
Adorn'd a Countess with that Name ;
Whose Wit surmounting firmly stood,
All Creatures with a Riding-hood.

Her Lord for Treason all deter,
Who had been dead were't not for her ;
King, Lords and Commons doom'd his Fate,
The Tower his Goal, the Warders set,
Petitions could no Mercy draw,
And Ladies Tears Impeached the Law ;
All this the *Heroine* withstood,
And baffled by a Riding-hood.

Saturnia gave with Closing Light
The Criminal, his last sad Night.
When th' Sprightly Countess did the Deed,
She weept, she had all in her Head.
She dress'd her Lord, inform'd his Mind,
Made Soldiers dumb, and Warders blind ;
And all the Nation prais'd her Mood,
For the Inchanted Riding-hood.

In spite of Ears, in spite of Eyes
Of Power and Wealth, that Crowns our Joys,
This Rarity of Women's Mould,
With female Jerking then Controwl'd
The great Lieutenant bold and Gay,
That has good Judgment, as some say,
Must think his prudent part not good,
Out-witted by a Riding-hood.

Observe this Rule, you that have Power,
From *Newgate's* Mansion to the *Tower*,
No more ingage with Female Wit,
Nor seek to find out their Deceit:

For take this grave Advice from me,
You shall not hear, you shall not see,
Till they their rare Design make good,
As now they've done the Riding-hood.

Let Traitors against Kings conspire,
Let secret Spies great Statesmen hire,
Nought shall be by Detection got,
If Women may have leave to Plot :
There's nothing clos'd with Bars or Locks
Can hinder Nightrayls, Pinners, Smocks,
For they will every one make good,
As now they've done the Riding-hood.

Oh thou, that by this Sacred Wife
Hast sav'd thy Liberty and Life,
And by her Wits immortal Pains,
With her quick Head hast sav'd thy Brains :
Let all Designs her Worth Adorn,
Sing her an Anthem Night and Morn,
And let thy fervent Zeal make good
A Reverence for the Riding-hood.

An Epilogue *to* Henry *the Second;* Intended for *Rosamond.*

IN this Grave Age, Improv'd by Statesmen's Art,
   What hopes have I, that you should like my part;
Time was, when *Rosamond*, might shine at Court;
These are no Days for Misses of my Sort;
Your Bags for better Uses are prepar'd,
Beauty must now retrench, the Times are hard,
Whilst what should be a Bounty for the fair,
Is sav'd to beat the *French* in vig'rous War.
Had they expected something should be got
Our Scriblers sure, had chose another Plot;
And not thus heedlessly have found Occasion
To shew again the Grievance of a Nation.
All Mistresses were long since left in th' Lurch
You Lovers now are fighting for your Church;
Saints Militant, who devoutly have agreed,
To stand by Doctrine that you never read.
How strangely Time does Human things decay,)
Four Centurys past, as Ancient Writers say,   }
She that I represent, bore mighty Sway:)
Her Beauty wonder'd at, her Wit Extoll'd:
Her yellow Locks were call'd, too, Threads of Gold,
But now should that Complexion use the Trade,)
Each little Fop the Town has newly made,   }
Would Cry, Confound the Carrot Pated Jade.)
A Miss in Days of War and Jeopardy,)
Like Armourers in Times of Peace must be }
Their Swords and Helmets rust, and so will she.)
What sort of Criticks then shall I endear,
To favour my abandon'd Character?
The *French* fatigue too much to mind Amour;
The *German* bigotted, the *Spaniard* poor;
The *Belgick* Lover, with his Northern Sense;
Would have the *Yofrow*, but would spare the Pence,
Ravenous of Beauty, but when Purse should open,
Myn Heer is either deaf or Drunk *a stopen;*

Y 2

Thus

'Thus o'er all *Europe*, as the Scenes are laid,
War and Religion have quite spoil'd Love's Trade ;
Since then from Court, my part must hope no Pity,
I'll try the *English* Lovers in the City ;
Kind Souls, who many a Night o'er Toast and Ale ;
Have wept at Reading *Rosamond's* fam'd Tale ;
And will, I hope, for Beauty's sake to Day ;
Confront these Beaus, and save an honest Play.
So may you Thrive, your Wagers all be won ;
So may your wise Stock-jobbing Crimp go on,
So may your Ships return from the Canaries,
And no damn'd *Dunkirk* Shark snap up their *Johns*
    and *Marys*,
Stand Buff once for a Mistress, think what lives
Some of you daily Live with Scolding Wives ;
For though I fell by Jealous Cruelty,
For venial Sin, 'twas pity I should dye ;
Ah ! should your Wives and Daughters so be try'd, ⎫
And with my Dose their failings purify'd   ⎬
Lord, what a Massacre would maul *Cheapside!*   ⎭

A PROLOGUE,

At the Opening of the Play house, Spoken by Young Powel.

A Tragick Scene of Woe, which long did last,
   Has Acted been this fatal Winter past ;
This, on the World's great Stage, all find too true,
Ours, the Epitome, resents it too
With double Grief, for th' general Loss, and you :
Besides, strange Jarrs, are now amongst us grown,
One Mischief very seldom comes alone :
Strifes are pursued with such Impetuous Rage,
The *Muses* dread the downfal of the Stage ;
Our Grandees too, that wrangling Cases try,
Fatten with Feuds, but starve the lesser Fry :
To you, we therefore (the poor forlorn) Petition,
You only can relieve our sad Condition,
And save us from the Wrack of their Division ;
Whilst they for Rights and Titles hotly strive,
In different Partys, and Rencounter drive,
We would but Live, we dare not think to Thrive :
Let not their Quarrels push our Ruin on,
Pray let us be too Mean to be undone ;
When the Finny Warriors of the Ocean made
A scaly War, a watry Cavalcade ;
The great one's the fierce Combat did endure,
The Smelts and petty Prawns were all secure.
The Ladys Smile, thence I date good Success,
Smiles look most lovely in a Mourning Dress ;
And you our Patrons, tho' your Habits shew
The solemn Mode, yet wear no Cloudy Brow :
Tho' outward Sables seem like gloomy Night,
Your Pockets Argent, comforts us like Light,
Money has Rays superlatively bright ;
And whilst with that our heavy Hearts you cheer,
In any Colour you are welcome here :

Ah,

Ah ! would your favour Diligence befriend,
We'd strive to please, and every Minute mend,
Pray use no Rod, before we do offend ;

For tho', as formerly (when we all joyn'd
To make Wit's Banquet proper to your Mind)
We can't in such fine Dishes bring our Cates,
We'll serve ye up a pretty Treat in Plates ;
Some Actors we have still, some New ones got,
Young Tits extreamly willing to be taught,
A silly Bashfulness is all their fault :

That once Remov'd, as in our hopeful Clime,
They'll soon Instructed be in Prose or Rhime,
No doubt' the Girls will come to good in Time ;
But as they are, if Truth must be express'd,
They Caw, and Gape, like Birds just fledg'd
    in th' Nest,
And Blush at the meer hinting of a Jest.

You lik'd new Faces Sirs, not long ago,
Pray come and see these, try what they can do ;
For tho' an Actress, if I take it right,
Can't like a Mushroom sprout up in a Night ;
Yet if you influence her Inclination,
She may divert with other Conversation :
However, we shall always play our Parts,
Industriously strive to gain your Hearts ;
With utmust Diligence your Pleasure serve,
Nor spare our Pains, but study to deserve.

An

An EPILOGUE,

For Mrs. VERBRUGGAN.

PISH, I had e'en as good go out again,
  I see our Fate, you are in your Damming Vein ;
And every Critick looks so like a Devil,
'Twill be Time lost, to beg you to be Civil :
Yet hang't, I'll try for once, what I can say,
'Twill be at worst, but a Speech thrown away ;
Thus then I sue to all, Dukes, Lords, Knights & Squires,
Gentlemen, Jokers, sellers of Wit, and buyers :
Beaus of the Court, and Bullys of the Fryers,
True Wits, and no Wits, Tartars tilting Heroes,
Poets, Pimps, Prentices, and poor Piacros ;
Sharks, Shagrags, Shatter-brains, Panders, Purse-takers,
Citts, Country Cullys, Cuckolds, Cuckold-makers :
All you that in this lower Row are Noted,
And you that yonder are so high Promoted ;
Be pleas'd to lay your thumping Anger by,
And spare the Carkass of the Comedy :
You too the charming Sex, Ladies well known,
You that have Titles, you too that have none ;
You in whose youthful Cheeks the Blood does lye,
And you that use fine Tinctures to supply :
Fortunes high flyers, you that mount our Boxes,
And you low Tire, Cracks, Harridans and Doxies ;
Of all Degrees, a favour I implore,
Old young, fat lean, straight, crooked, rich or poor :
That you would curb the Humour in to Day,
And for this once like an indifferent Play ;
Not for its Merit, can I beg your Grace,
But only for my Sake, pray let it pass :
Consider faith, how hard it is to please,
And how unequal each Man's Humour is ;
Just as the present Weather, that we see,
Now treats our Spring, you treat our Poetry :
When you should kindly Rain, you roughly blow,
And when your Sun should shine on us, you Snow ;

Blast

Blast all our Buds, when you should clear and warm,
And when your Breezes should refresh, you Storm :
Some fancys Rhiming Plays to Mirth provoke,
Others there are that like a smutty Joke ;
That way my Talent lies, if I have any,
And will I hope Diversion give to many :
But to please all, one Woman can't ingage,
Tho' the best Actress that e'er trod the Stage.

A PROLOGUE.

For CAVE UNDERHILL.

THE humerous Author of this comick Play,
    Gives me the Name of *Jollyman* to Day ;
And some Years since, in good King *Charles's* Reign,
Who Wit and Womens Right did well maintain :
When Courtiers, and almost all other folks,
Kissing and tipling liv'd the Life of Ducks ;
'Tis known, tho' now there's one Leg in the Grave,
Mankind in general call'd me Jolly *Cave* :
The Women too, thought me a proper Fellow,   ⎫
Well limb'd, tho' Phiz was bord'ring upon Yellow, ⎬
And pleasant, tho' oft tempted to be mellow ;   ⎭
Then Audiences too were seldom thin,   ⎫
My Action from the Court Applause could win,   ⎬
The Pit would laugh, the upper Gallerys grin : ⎭

But long was I not blest, e'er I miscarry'd,
I play'd my worst part of a Fool, I Marry'd ;
A Wife must settle, with a Murrain to me,
The only solid Curse, that could undo me :
But she an easy Life best to secure,
At last chang'd for a better, much good do her ;
And left me here, Prince of true Comedy,
To reap the Fruits of your Civility,

                                        I've

I've strove to reap, but barren is the Mould,
Besides my Hook is rusty grown, and old :
In Soil not well Manur'd, no Grain will grow,
How should I reap, alass, unless you Sow ?
And whether the kind Crop will hold out well,
This Day I think does but too sadly tell :
Yet one thing makes me laugh, tho' Wit and Sence, ⎫
And pleasing Humour is quite gone from hence,   ⎬
And Foreign *Sol fa*, grubbles up the Pence ;   ⎭

Tho' all the Beaus are from our Boxes fled,
And our two Houses scarce can get us Bread :
A third is building to insult our Woes,
But who will fill't, the Lord of *Oxford* knows ;
As for the Masques, my old Acquaintance there,
They have my Acting try'd before, elsewhere,
Applause from them at least I shall procure
Their Claps are very frequent, that I'm sure ;
Only this comfort still there's left in store, ⎫
I'll labour to refine the ruggid Ore,   ⎬
I'll strive to please, and wish I cou'd do more. ⎭

A PROLOGUE.

For the BASSET-TABLE.   *Spoken by Mr.* PINKETHMAN, *acting a Footman in a Lac'd Livery.*

OUR Poetess, designing to expose,
    The Gaming Vice, amongst the Bel's and Beaus ;
T'illustrate wisely her dramatick Art,
Has strove to hit my fancy, in my part :
For tho' you think my Figure now a Jest, ⎫
'Mongst all Imployments, in the Town possest, ⎬
A Footman's and a Drawer's, I think are best ; ⎭
The Drawer as he supports the Toping vice,
By force your Bounty does monopolize :

And

And tho' the Reck'ning be five Pound, or ten,)
If there's no Spill allow'd besides for *Ben,*   }
Y'are surely Poison'd if you come again ;   )
His Days are gainful, by your Idle Hours,   )
I knew a Drawer, from hence not many Doors,   }
That kept two Geldings, and a Leash of Whores :)
Thus getting the Ascendant o'er your Brains,
The Man increases, tho' the Master wains ;
Like his, the Footman's happy state is try'd,
But then, 'tis true, he must be qualify'd :
A jantee Air, a bold assuring Face,
And must be a good Pimp, in the first place ;
Then likewise, as in Trust he higher grows,)
Must know a Dun, with genuine suppose,   }
As Spannels do their Masters, by the Nose :)
Who if he knocks, and asks, and asks again,
The cue is ready, *Sir, he's not within ;   * *Alt'ring his*
When 'Squire above, sits Shivering in the cold, (*Voice.*
Numb'ring the change of the last piece of Gold :
Cards, he must know too, and to cog a Dye,
He may spare Swearing, but must naturally Lye ;
With mean beginning Grandeur oft is nurst,
The greatest Rivers were small Springs at first :
And as the scribling Clark does often vary,)
Rising by Fate, to Mr. Secretary,   }
From thence to Office Extraordinary ;   )
So *John* the Footman, from Industrious use)
Of shaking Flambeau, and of cleaning Shoes ; }
Steps to be Butler, from whose sprightly Juice)
He Steward turns, then carrying all before him,
Is made soon after Justice of the *Quorum ;*
Things being thus, spite of this † Pye bald geer,
This Ominous Cord, upon my Shoulders here :
And other Equipage ‖ this part to Day,   )
I like as well, as any in the Play,   }
And if you please to laugh at me, you may.   )

---

† *Pointing to his lac'd Coat.*   ‖ *Lac'd Hat.*

The FABLE

Of the LADY, *the* LURCHER, *and the Mar-
row-*PUDDINGS.   *Aluding with Topical
hints to some late Senatorical Occurrences.*

IN Days when Birds and Beasts did prate,
   And human Understanding own ;
A Lyoness in *Parthia* late,
Who had a plentiful Estate,
   There liv'd in great Renown.

Well stor'd with Lands and Tenements,
And was for Riches and for Rents,
   By various Suitors follow'd ;
She still with all things Treated well,
But *Marrow-Puddings* in her Cell,
   The best that e'er were swallow'd.

For which her Guests were seldom few,
The Four legg'd Brutes, and those with Two,
   Came thick as 'twere for Places ;
But 'mongst the crowd that made their Courts,
The Race of *Dogs*, as Fame reports,
   Stood best in her good Graces.

My great Lord Mastiff, round and squat,
And lank Sir Greyhound soon grew fat,
   The *Puddings* nourish'd rarely ;
Neat Spanniel 'Squires and combing Shocks,
With deep mouth'd Jowlers too, and Rocks,
   Were at her Leve early.

Whence many went well pleas'd away,
Regail'd and pamper'd Sleek and gay,
   Most better fed than taught ;
One *Lurcher* only rough and lean,
With Acid Humours and the Spleen
   Had yet no *Pudding* got.

He

He being too voracious known,
Had soon devour'd all his own,
    At least all those of *Marrow;*
And being in a desp'rate case,
Long knew not how to help Distress,
    Nor how to Beg, or Borrow.

The Dame too, who right Merit weigh'd,
Knew no just cause he should be fed,
    Or fatten'd by her Bounty;
Who us'd to give by Barking, helps,
And was the Mouth of all the Whelps,
    Against her in the County.

Desert she knew, she oft had paid,
And some too *Marrow-Puddings* had,
    Tho' their pretence was small;
Which more inflames the *Lurcher's* care,
Who now resolves with them to share,
    Tho' he has none at all.

And to proceed in't, on a Time,
When *Phœbus* from the *East* did climb,
    To his Meridian Station;
Accosting one of his own Crew,
Whom he of the right Kidney knew,
    He thus begin's Narration.

A *Marrow-Pudding* 'mongst our Race,
You know's the same thing as a Place,
    'Mongst Humans by Court dunning;
And since the Dame so close is grown,
And thinks it fit to give me none,
    I'll make her do't by cunning.

Thou know'st my way of Barking well,
I'll give out such a hideous yell,
    Our Tribe oft urge me to it:
Shall give the Matron such small ease,
She shall not eat her Meat in Peace,
    She knows that I can do it.

And

And soon shall find by subtile Arts,
What 'tis to slight a Dog of Parts,
  Or when I sue, deny it;
For be my Reasons false or true,
I'll have a *Marrow-Pudding* too,
  Or she ne'er be at quiet.

I know she soon must keep a Court,
Where all her Tenants will resort,
  Her Steward too be there;
Whom with my din I'll so Torment,
I'll make 'em grudge to pay their Rent,
  And all their Leases tear.

I'll howl aloud to every one,
Who knows her that she is undone,
  Dire Ruin is her Lot;
Nay, I'll send Printed Scrowls beyond,
To Neighbours o'er the Herring Pond,
  That she's not worth a Groat.

And tho' my Country suffer in't,
Z—ns I shall see my Name in Print,
  By bellowing Hawkers cry'd;
Whilst by exposing thus my Wit,
The one gives a Revenge that's sweet,
  And t'other feeds my Pride.

I'll Bark that tho' we've taken *Lisle*,
Bruges and *Ghent*, with all the Spoil,
  And baulk'd the hot *Pretender;*
He's coming to renew his Claim,
With solid hopes t'affront the Dame,
  When no one will Defend her.

I'll Bark that all our Losses come,
From great Ones Treachery at home,
  Who hope to gain their ends;
And tho' our Conquests gain Renown,
The *Mounsieur's* not the weaker grown,
  VVhilst here he has such Friends.

I'll

I'll Bark that many Ships at Sea,
By Cowardice are made a Prey,
  To the aforesaid Neighbours;
That vile Deceit their Rulers sway,
And those who Contributions pay,
  Do all but lose their Labours.

I'll roar againt one Noble Peer,
With all my Tribe to prove it cleer,
  That he's the Nation's Curse;
I'll call him *Judas*, void of Grace,
A pox on Manners in this case,
  Because he bears the Purse.

And tho' the Dame's great Men at Arms,
Last Year gave *Mounsieur* such alarms,
  His Crown was thought unstable;
Her General's Glory I'll make less,
And Bark in spite of Services,
  We're all most Miserable.

I'll rail at all in noted rank,
But most severely 'gainst the Bank,
  The Pest of our Diseases;
Nay, I'll Invetreacy advance,
And swear the Bully Rock of *France*,
  Can break 'em when he pleases.

'Gainst *Northern* great Ones held to Bail,
I'll whet my Tongue and loudly rail,
  In a most hedious Tone;
And swear tho' we don't hit the blots,
Their Treason was amongst the *Scots*,
  Yet they were let alone.

And lastly I'll discourage all,
Who bring the Bags to *Grocers Hall*,
  By a subtle Play;
Whilst I'm insinuating a Fear,
Of *Mounsieur's* Second coming here,
  I'm guiding him the way.

I'll

I'll Howl against her Favourites,
Denouncing one there is that gets,
　　Heaps, to immense degree ;
Nor shall I fail to gain my ends,
For when I've Bark'd off all her Friends,
　　She must take up with me.

Thus did the *Lurcher* vent his Mind,
Nor fail'd, but what he had design'd,
　　He puts in Practice straight ;
The Lady and her best Allies,
Were daily vex'd with horrid noise,
　　And Nightly at her Gate.

The Times were bad by Fortunes course,
But he took pains to make 'em worse,
　　And every ill encrease ;
And tho' his bawling did no good,
Till *Pudding* in Possession stood,
　　Resolv'd it should not cease.

Whilst she with general good to all,
Scarce gave one Hour an interval,
　　VVithout indulgent care :
Tho with Seraphick Patience blest,
VVould often enquire what the Beast,
　　Meant to be so severe.

Her Friends to answer her Complaint,
Told her, a *Marrow-Pudding's* want,
　　Had made him late grow bolder ;
And yet they could not stint his noise,
Because the Creature had a Voice,
　　As being a Freeholder.

But that there would be matter soon,
The Scandal of his Tongue to prune,
　　If once more he harangu'd ;
And that ill Manners be reform'd,
He should for the past fault be VVorm'd,
　　And for the next be H—d.

A PROLOGUE.

To the KING *at the* Masque *at Court.*

WHen Wit and Science flourish'd in their Bloom,
   Combin'd to grace the State of ancient *Rome;*
Thus shon the Court from Peace, thus Pleasure sprung,
And thus * *Augustus* look'd, when *Ovid* sung:
Joy uncontroul'd and free possest each Mind,
And with good Humour, Loyalty was joined;
Instructive Poetry was nobly prais'd,
Dull Ignorance scorn'd, and artful Merit rais'd:
Thus *Cæsar's* smile each Genius did sublime,
And thus does our Inspirer bless our Time;
Thro' Clouds of anxious State and regal Care,
Shine out to make the Muses Region fair.
Sing then ye Sons of Wit and Harmony,
The Theme is glorious, raise your Voices high;
Renown, the happy Omen, Arts are grac'd,
And the glad Kingdom, consequently bless'd:
Let joyful *Britains* grateful Thanks ne'er cease,
Restor'd to her Religion, and her Peace,
In spite of Native sullen Humour, own
The wondrous Work, as wonderously done;
Yet should Ingratitude vile Parties sway,
Apollo's Race shall constant Duty pay,
And from Oblivion's Rust secure that glorious Day;
Let Malecontents in Joy be tardy found,
The Muses loyal Song shall give perpetual Sound,
And spacious *Europe's* Happiness proclaim,
In her immortal Arbitrators Fame.

  Let rash tarpawling *Czars* swell future Story,
By surreptitious Ways of seeking Glory;
With sly Designs, tho' like themselves, half froze,
From *Russian* Isicles, *Muscovian* Snows,
Sneak here to learn how our Ship-forest grows;

---

* *Bowing to the King.*

To

To glean fall'n Ears of *England's* Grandeur come,
And make a fancy'd Harvest on't at home ;
Let th' Savage Race, their Furrs about their Ears,
Scarcely distinguish'd from their Native Bears,
With crowds Undisciplin'd cause petty Fears.
The Maiden Charge of one young Brave Allie,
O'th' Lion strain, tho' we aloof stand by,
To Holes can make the filching Foxes fly :
So one Young *Ammon*, with a well Train'd few,
Did *Persian* Ignorance in Shoals subdue.
　　Let our aspiring Neighbour too forget
His solemn Act, when *Europe's* Councel met ;
'Gainst Right and Honour let Ambition plead,
And pull more Curses on his Hoary-head :
Let him the Breach of Royal Faith think wise,
And shame a King with base *Plebian* Vice.
Blest *Albion's* Guardian, fated to redress
Injurious Ills, wherever they oppress ;
Prompted by Justice soon to *Austrian* Land,
Could fierce as *Jove*, reach his deciding Hand :
And as of late, when War's rude Tempest reign'd,
The Royal Umpire their sunk State maintain'd :
When *Mammon* that in Golden Ingots shines,
Undug lay useless in their *Western* Mines.
　　Britannick Vertue, where true Valour lyes,
Inspir'd our glorious Troops to fight their Prize :
That Vertue once revers'd, their Sails can lower,
And fix in juster Hands their lawless Power ;
Ah ! would our Patriots their Feuds give o'er,
And make true use of their extensive Pow'r :
Fit Aids without a Niggard's Caution give,
Advise the King, not touch Prerogative :
Do publick Justice without private Picks,
For th' general, not by Ends, learn Politicks :
Would they with moderate Calmness make Report,
Their Country serve without Offence at Court ;
Councel, not curb, stretch, and not break the strings,
In short would they be Senates, and not Kings ;
If twenty Infant Dukes abroad should Reign.
As many perjur'd Sires, his Spurious Right maintain :

Whilst the old Bulwark *Ocean* round us runs,
If Union arm'd the Hearts of *Britain's* Sons,
'Twould still be in our Pow'r, to right each wrong,
And crush the Viper e'er he grew too strong :
But this, oh *Albion !* is too great a Grace,
Too rich a Cordial for thy squeamish Race.
Instead of Concord, needless Doubts and Fears,
Deludes thy Sence, malicious Lyes thy Ears :
The various Weather just thy Humour hits,
Now hot, now cold, it storms and shines by fits,
And grave State-menders now sprout up from Cits.
The Apron Tribe with Politicks are stor'd
And every *Coffee Room's* a Council board ;
Where Publick News in Print each Day's convey'd,
And all Court Mystery's are open lay'd :
This Man's a Lord, the King perhaps ne'er thought on,
T'other a Place has given him, or has bought one ;
Such Courtiers mov'd, such Captains by are lay'd,
Disbanded too, e'er they're so much as pay'd :
On this straight all degrees discanting prate,
And Canvass grand *Arcana's* of the State :
The Taylor with Grub Beard, and Crimson Nose,
The King and Parliament together sows :
The Snipsnap Barber, lathering *Spain's* Condition,
Severely marks the breadth of the Partition :
The Cutler swears more Troops well Arm'd should
    meet,
The Cropeard Cobler stitches up the Fleet ;
And all the rest, as Interest sways the Mood,
Rail on, or Praise, pretending general Good ;
The *Muses* only Tribe unbyass'd joyn,
Recording Good and Ill, without design ;
Great Heroes Actions Sing, for little gain,
And Earn a trifling Praise with solid Pain :
If with Dramaticks we to please pretend :
We're said to sooth the Vices we should mend,
The Zealous Crew from *Tubs*, bark senceless Fury,
And th' dullest of all Cuckolds, a *Grand Jury :*
Or else the absolving Hypocrite stands by,
And drolling Mirth makes Immorality ;

Stage

Stage Wantonness, a Damning fault is shewn,
But Treason and Rebellion must be none;
Well then since Spight, not Zeal, this Reprehension
    draws,
We to a higher Court remove our Cause:
We may have Errors, and may Errors mend,
When just Reproof is given us like a Friend;
As spots in Stars, so faults in Wit may be,
But Faction or Rebellious Villany;
The Loyal *Muse* ne'er taint, aloft she sings,
On Themes of Glory and Immortal things;
Fame's deathless Race, as far as Heaven renown'd,
And whilst *Apollo* smiles, her Joys are Crown'd.

A PROLOGUE,

Made to Entertain her ROYAL HIGHNESS,
at Her coming to the Play, call'd, IBRA-
HIM 13, *Emperor of the* Turks.   *Spoken
by Mrs.* CROSS.

EACH Critick here, methinks, puts on a Face, ⎫
  As when in Prologues in my Childish Days, ⎬
I was sent simp'ring out to sue for Grace: ⎭
When I was forc'd, (to get the House some Guineas)
To Praise for Wits, a Pit half full of Ninnys;
But Sparks, those Poppet Hours are wasted now, ⎫
I'll Sneak and Cringe no more—I'd have you know, ⎬
I've more respect for my Fourteen then so. [*Proudly.* ⎭
If you believe it, you'll not find me apt,
I am not now so fond of being Clapt:
More Years, more Knowledge—And for all your
    Humming,
Look to't, ye Beaus, my Fifteen is a coming.
That happy Age, which you so dearly prize,
I'm pleas'd to think, how I shall Tyrannize;

                                    For

For I intend to Murder—Kill and Slay,
An Army of Young Coxcombs every Day:
'Tis Comical to tell how two short Years,
Alters the Turn and Shape of my Affairs.
In those Days, a Pert, Modish, Mealy Fop,
White as a Sack in a Corn-chandler's Shop,
Us'd to Perfume with Snuff our Dressing-Rooms,
And Treat me—As most fit—With Sugar-Plumbs,
But now Smiles, Struts—Looks in my Eyes—and
    Combs ;
Whispers for Secrets, what I knew long since,
And further of strong Passion to convince.
The soft Court-Tongue, crys—'Gad,* it does adore me,
And Feather Blue—Veils its Campaign—† before me.
But this shan't do, Sirs,—My reserv'd Behaviour
Shall shew ye now, I'll not provoke your Favour,
Nor feed ye with false Hopes—To gain a Smile,
But to the Darling Genius of our Isle,
I turn my Duty, as I change my Stile.
Madam, At your Blest Feet, her Prostrate Muse,
The Author lays———And for your Favour sues :
Your Presence fills her with so true a Joy,
'Tis not in Criticks Power to destroy.
Ill-natur'd Envy cloudy Censure bears,
But Fogs still vanish, when the Sun appears.
Now pleas'd, the *Helliconian* Dwellers sing,
To see your *Highness* Consecrate their Spring,
And *Pegasus* prepares to mount the Wing.
To Celebrate through Heaven, and Earth, and Sea,
The Sacred Patroness of Poetry.

---

    * *Speaking affectedly.*   † *Speaking roughly.*

A

A PROLOGUE,

Spoken by a Comedian who lately left the Irish Theater, *at his return thither.*

AS some Deserter mutining for Pay, }
Who rashly has from Colours gone astray,
Spying by chance a Gallows in his way ;
The fatal Object terrifying his sight,
Returns with Shame, back to his Post to Fight :
So I, on thought of you———
Back to my Comick Post again dispatch me ;
E'er the vile sound of Renegado reach me
Or the dire Halter of your Anger catch me ;
Which would inflict my Punishment much more,
Having so oft, your Favours found before :
But know, 'twas not to slight your generous Love,
I've thus Elop'd, but only to improve :
I thought I wanted something, so sheer'd off,
To stock me with new Whims, to make ye laugh ;
And as the Country sordid rich Wiseacres,
Who dully think all Foreigners Man-makers,
Send out their Booby Sons to *France*, to Dress,
Or to suck Doctrine from his Holiness :
So I to practice the true Playhouse Maggot,
Have been initiating, I ought to brag it,
In *London* Town, with *Pinkethman* and *Dogget.*
For your Diversion, thus I've taken care,
And brought ye o'er a Sample of their Ware,
Not that the *Muses* flourish more than here.
For they're still Witty at their own Expence,
A Pound of Faction, to an ounce of Sence ;
But to regale ye with some new Grimaces,
Queint ways of speaking Jokes, and making Faces ;
In which to please ye, I'll my best employ,
Incourag'd to't this time of general Joy ;
A time when you, your long'd for Hopes obtain,
Whilst lasting Bliss crowns your brave Viceroy's
And *Albion's* loss is blest *Hibernia's* gain.   [Reign,

An

An EPILOGUE.

For Mrs. LUCAS.

Y'HAVE seen me Dance, and ye have heard me
   Sing,
But now I'm put upon another thing;
By way of *Epilogue* to make a Speech,
If I can Frame my Mouth for't, I'm a Witch:
Nor that I find there's ought that can Provoke in't,
But should there chance to be a smutty Joke in't,
Any Reflection, or the least word of Bawdy,
That should disgust a Gentleman, or Lady:
What case were I in then, what Desolation?
Would that be to my Virgin Reputation?
A great huge Girl, to blirt out a Paw word,
Nay, tho' twere Privileg'd and on Record:
I would not such a Thing, by me were said,
For fifty Pistoles, as I am a Maid.
Or should the Plaguy *Poet* in his Rhimes,
Give some unlucky bob upon the Times;
As————Heaven help us, those that use his way,
In this fine World————May have enough to say;
And so to punish me for Faults, are his,
I should be fetch'd to come upon my Knees:
Me——On my Knees! amongst a throng this Weather,
Ivads no————I an't such a Baby neither;
So I'll speak none on't————But say I'm asham'd,
And let him take his Paper————And be Damn'd:
I'm for no Jerking *Epilogues*, not I,   }
Unless the words are chopt—Like Mince-meat for }
 a Pye,   }
But stay, since honest *Bourdon* here stands by,
And that I may more handsomely get rid on't,
We'll sing the last new* Dialogue instead on't.

---

* *Sings and* Exit.

                    A

A PROLOGUE.

IN the first happy Golden Age,
When solid Wit and Judgment deck'd the Stage;
Heroes and Poets bore an equal Grace,
The Victor's Oak still flourish'd with the Bayes;
Whilst Arts with Arms united, did sublime,
A spacious Series of succeeding time;
But you of Glorious modern Race, now get
Preheminence, and bear the Prize from Wit:
Each Day performing some Triumphant thing,
Beyond the Genius of the Muse to Sing;
Witness late bravery on *Castillian* Strand,
Where through the foaming Waves ye Swam to Land,
Your Foes dire Fate still glittering in each Hand.
Witness your Heats and Colds, and Hardships there,
Which following your great Leader—You could bear;
With more than Mortal Patience, tho' among,
The pangs of scorching blasts which Griefs prolong,
And swarms of starv'd Muskeitoirs, which like Hor-
    nets stung.
Who hourly plagu'd—Charm'd by some *Popish* Saints,
Th' undisciplin'd Corps of each good *Protestants;*
Witness at *Vigo* too, the *Mounsieur's* Doom,
The well-pac'd Toyl of bringing *Galleons* home,
The Glorious storming of the Fort and breaking
    of the Boomb.
Then to crown all, let our Land-Forces take,
The freshest Garland Goddess Fame can make;
Pegasus flags, too low to mount the praise,
Which our brave General's Renown shall raise:
For which the Belgians—Trophys should advance,
Turn Orators, nay Wits——In scorn of *France,*
And drink his Health——
With shoals of pickled Herrings in a Sea of *Nants:*
But leaving them their ways of Gratitude,
Let proper Duty be by us pursu'd;
Welcome then all ye noble *British* Sons,
Brave Strangers too, who late have scourg'd the Dons:
                                   Whose

Whose Valour puts a stop to *Gallick* Fame,
Whilst wavering *Portugal* comes in for shame ;
Welcome to *England*, to your Native Shore,
Honour'd with Science—But with Valour more :
Ah ! could my Wishes your Deserts pursue,   ⎫
As you have Praise——You had got Plunder too,   ⎬
Your *Jesuits* Bark had prov'd a Golden bough.   ⎭
The Campaign Snuff, which every Box incloses,
Had turn'd Gold Dust, to gratifie your Noses,
For well I know, tho' Honour's the main story,
A little Gain suits well a little Glory :
Courage improves, when Fortune's open handed,
I'm sure I should think so if I Commanded ;
For 'tis past doubt, not the kind Maid undrest,
With flowing Hair, bright Eyes and Snowy Breast :
To her hot Lover can be thought so dear,
Nor to the famish'd Glutton lusty chear ;
Not Gold to the Mitre, Flattery to the Proud,
Gay dress to Beauty——Faction to the Crow'd :
Attracts the Soul——Nor half so much does Charm,
As luscious Plunder, when a Town we Storm ;
But Sirs, I hope that good amends is mking,
In the now design'd *West-India* Undertaking :
That Colonels, Captains, and the rest will find,
The Golden Fleece, Fate for the brave design'd ;
Nay, th' Vulgar too—You Lads—Each honest Fellow,
That sit there—Cloth'd in Grey, Blue, Green and
        Yellow :
List but your selves among the Grenadiers,
No more Hoof beating——Banish all those fears,
But home next Winter come, and ride in Chairs.

An EPILOGUE *for Mrs.* VERBRUGGAN.

AT this odd Time of Bustle and of hurry,
   'Tis wonderful to find ye Sirs so merry;
Why, see now what a Country Lass can do,
When would they e'er be tickled so by you* ?
You that are plying for Sheepbiters here,
And hope to sell your Mutton Loyns so dear :
No, no, those Rampant Days are gone good Folk,
Your *India* Ware's forbid, your *China's* broke,
Or if some little Sport, should their wise Heads pro-
    voke,
Some Freeholder's fresh Spouse, some Rosebush *Dolly*
Must do't, no *Covent-Garden Trolly Lolly;*
Your Pardon Gentlemen, for my blunt Jest,
I take ye all for Patriots at least :
I know they're chosen all the Nation o'er,
From the *Lands End*, home to our Churches door;
Where lately trudging to make sound and whole,
Some broken matters, that concern'd my Soul,
A Grave face ask'd me, if I came to——Poll.
To Poll cry'd I—What's that—As hot as Embers ?
Zoons Mistress, said he bluff, to give your Vote for
    Members :
I Blush'd, for as I'm a right Homespun Lady,
I thought the Man had Jeer'd me—And spoke Bawdy;
Ha, ha, ha, ha——Well I'll again to School,
Ads life a Player——Yet be such a Fool :
That's pretty——For with my Poetick Gleanings,
I sure might know that Word had several Meanings :
Without Instruction——By your Pardon——Pray,
And from henceforward every one in's way :
I'll leave th' hard Word for you, when y'are together,
And study merry Jokes, 'gainst you come hither;
With Comick Mirth I'll calm your Jarring strain,
And shew in Farce, some *Frenchified* hot Brain :
That pause in his Credentials, brought in vain,
That *England* sooner will be *France* retaking,
Than take a Master of their Master's making.

------

* *Pointing to the Vizard Masks.*

A

A PROLOGUE.

For Estcourt's *Benefit Day.*

Enter Pinkethman *finely Drest, pushing in* Lee *before him, Drest like a Fat Fellow.*

To make a Prologue, *we've two Seasons chose,*
'Tis New and Comical we may suppose,
Pray listen Ladys, pray be silent Beaus.

Pin. ON *Estcourt's* Day, and to such Company, ⎫
      Dare you Pricquister *Prologue* speak with ⎬
      me,   ⎭

Lee. Leanman, I dare——And do't *Extempore.*

P. Good, what's your Subject—What will you be ?
    For my own part I'll chuse——Stay let me see ;
    Come——I'll be *Lent*, as Lean as a starv'd Rat,

L. Than I'll be *Easter*——Jolly, Fair and Fat :

P. Proceed then come, me *Lent* begins the Jest,

L. And let the Audience hear whose hint is best :
    We'll make our Speeches, let them judge the whole,
    I for the Body argue,

P. I the Soul.   *Hum*   [*Pauses.*
    Lent was ordain'd, to leave our Sins i'th' lurch,
    There's for you Rogue, that never go to Church ;

L. You can't make proof of that, nor any Man,
    And so pray mind your Text Friend and go on ;

P. *Lent* still is dear to him, good life that leads, ⎫
    To the true *Protestant* that Prays and Reads, ⎬
    And *Popish* Saints, that rattle o'er their Beads. ⎭

L. *Easter* comes briskly in—When *Lent* is gone—
    First nimbly chears us with the dancing *Sun :*
    The *Sun*, that we suppose by ancient story,
    To be the first that ever Danc'd a Boree ;

P. Flesh, *Lent* debars us in each Houshold dish, ⎫
    What's wholesome should be grateful to our wish, ⎬
    Our very Consciences—Should be all—Fish ; ⎭

                                            And

And taught by Rules that Decency does bring,
Bear part with good fresh Cod, and fragrant Ling :
L. Easter for jolly chear more Praise deserves,
Indulging these, Penurious *Lent* half Starves ;
In *Easter* time we sit with Female Cousins,
And Cakes and Custards, swallow down by Dozens :
P. Then *Lent* does weekly give two Holidays,
For all that will be Good, to make Essays,
Keeps also from the Town two wicked Plays ;
Where Fops and Strumpets, and Mohocks might be,
L. And Rakehells, just like *Pinkethman*
P. And *Lee.*
Lent, from all Seasons of the Year does vary,
Keeps back the forward Ass—Resolv'd to Marry ;
Thus may Young Wiseacres, advantage reap,
And timely learn to Look before they Leap :
That trouble mayn't by a rash Act appear,
And dire Repentance close the ending Year :
L. Ah—How much better *Easter* does provide,
When Doubts are vanisht, for the buxome Bride ;
When tedious Time has fixt the happy Day,
Lover sticks close—And Mamma says you may :
Late Fasting meals allows but slender Food,
Some Flesh now Child will do thy Stomach good :
P. Well, well, for all your sly and Roguish Rhime,
If vulgar things may mix with those sublime,
For Fishmongers and Parsons, *Lent's* the time ;
The first grows Rich by vending watry Diet,
As the last by Preachments—Little for our Quiet :
L. If Fishmongers so lucky you affirm,
Zoons what are Lawyers in an *Easter* Term ;
Who buz like Bees—'Till they go laden home,
And smiles to find their Time of Roguery come.

A Prologue *Spoken like a* Scotch High-
    lander *with a Sword and Target*.

I Am a Thing, yet drest in *Northern* Clothing,
  A Man my say as I appear, I'm nothing;
Yet late at angry *Preston*——Stoutly taking,
The Rebels part I came, a new King making:
Held up my Target, for that Blustring trash,
Surnam'd the bold *Maclando MACKINTOSH;*
Some we would have pack'd off, some here remain, ⎫
The Crucifixes are a peaceful Train,   ⎬
They've little in their Hands—But much in Brain: ⎭
Proud *Preston*, 'till 'twas Plunder'd by the Rout, ⎫
To make new *Saints*, drop'd fragrant Beads about, ⎬
But when bold *Wills* came in—Woons we went out; ⎭
Down went my broad Sword—Here's my Coat—To
      charge,
And a new Song to save me—Of *K. George:*   *Song.*
What 'tis we Play, is Song and Dance, and Shew,
The Theme, the Devil take me if I knew;
Yet this I dare affirm 'gainst all Bravadoes,
Our Songs will baulk the *Latin Nicoladoes:*
Here's Sence and Humour, and with free Twangdilloes,
We shall not choak ye with *Italian* Trilloes;
And as for me if I don't make ye Laugh,
You're Sick of the Catarrah, and of the Cough:
The *Hay-Market* does jingle to incite me,
Sirrah go fetch my Cloak—The Cold does fright me;
All Nonregardoes like my Female Noise,
They've Money, and can pay my squeaking Voice:
So in a Village have I seen a Clown,
With broken Noddle lay the Cudgels down;
And sneer to feel his Bloody mangled Scull,
As if the Blow had dignified the Fool.
But now 'tis plainer——'Tis a Loyal thing,
I turn my Quarters——And I praise the King:
    Hey, hey—Here's a Musical Lecture,
    To my Countrymen—[*Here several come in to hear,*
Ye Brittons *how long*, &c.

FINIS